MOVES

An MC Romance (Outlaw Souls Book 7)

HOPE STONE

GET FREE BOOKS!

Join Hope's newsletter to stay updated with new releases, get access to exclusive bonus content and much more!

Join Hope's newsletter here.

Tap here to see all of Hope's books.

Join Hope's Readers Group on Facebook.

MOVES

I heard the incessant whirring of my phone, sunken deep beneath the covers of my bed while I subconsciously tried to go back to sleep. Something clicked inside my mind, jolting me up while I fished around to retrieve it. I hurriedly answered it, waiting for it to connect after I'd listened to the voice of the operator asking me if I'd like to accept the charges.

"Hello?" I asked, trying not to sound as though I'd only just awoken.

"Hey, it's me," the voice on the other end of the line said, the connection of the call barely hanging on by a thread, but I recognized the voice. "I've gotten myself into a little bit of trouble here. Look, I've only got one phone call, and they're riding me pretty hard here. It's not often one of us gets pulled in like this. I'm sorry to ask, Moves, but I need your help,"

"You know I don't let people call me that anymore, Chalupa. When Padre died, I made everyone promise to stop calling me that, out of respect. Please honor that. I know you don't have much time, but I'll get you out. We're all family, remember?" I reminded him, knowing quite well that there would be no way I'd leave him behind.

"I'm sorry, and I know I shouldn't even bring this up, but do you even remember why Padre gave you the name 'Moves' in the first place?" I sighed, but I knew exactly what he was getting at.

"I do remember, Chalupa. It's been hard after his death is all," I confessed.

"I know, but I think you should keep it. Honor Padre with the name he gave, and make it mean something, man," said Chalupa, and I nodded my head on the other end of the line even though I knew he couldn't see me.

"Okay, you have a point. Now I want you to relax, all right? I'll be there to come get you as soon as I can," I replied.

"I'm just a little over my head here. I don't know what to do. I'm not going to last in prison, man." I could hear the fear in his voice, but I wasn't going to let it come to that.

"Whatever is going on, I'm going to get to the bottom of it. I need you to hang tight. They're not going to let you out of there until morning at least, so you stay strong, okay? I'll make sure you have a place to go once I get you out of that hellhole." My words seemed to calm him down a bit.

"Thank you, Moves," he said, hanging up the phone, and I could feel the reluctance through the line. I knew what it was like for him to be scared, especially because the police were always trying to ride our asses, and I could tell that he was far from innocent. I taught many of the men riding in the Outlaw Souls that we needed to cover our tracks, because the more we had the LPPD hounding us, the harder it would be to go about living our normal lives. I had faith that everything was going to be fine, but I needed to keep my head on straight, take care of a little business first before I managed to head back to bed.

I'm no use to Chalupa right now because they won't even let me post his bail this early.

I hated leaving him in there, but there's really nothing else I could do. I decided to head over to the small fridge in my dingy apartment, grab a beer, and head out back to give my bike a tune-up.

I wonder what they did with yours, Chalupa. There's no way we're gonna risk breaking it out if it's been impounded.

Looking down at the hunk of metal before me, I reminded myself that it was these bikes that bound us together for life. We were a family, and no amount of pain or grief was going to change that.

I wasn't the same person after I lost my parents, and I struggled to keep my head above water sometimes, especially now that the police were hot on our trail. I sat under the moonlight, feeling the cool air of approaching dawn brush against my skin while I got to work. I wiped the sweat off my forehead, making sure everything was in pristine condition before heading back inside to sleep off the rest of my frustration.

The Outlaw Souls had marked our territory in La Playa, and it was the only place that ever felt like home to me. No matter how much trouble we got ourselves into, how many drug deals went wrong, or how much money we lost, we always had each other's backs.

I had to make sure that I got Chalupa out of there before something bad happened. If the police had any solid evidence against him, this was going to be one hell of a ride.

I wondered what he could've done that led the police to his tail, but I could've already guessed. I worried that, with Chalupa locked up, there were going to be some members who were going to want to halt business until it was taken care of, but I wasn't sure that many of them knew what had happened.

It's probably best I keep things under wraps until I know for sure where all of this is headed.

I couldn't fall back asleep, my eyes catching sight of the steady stream of sunlight filtering in through the patched window in my bedroom while I tossed the covers aside, running my hand through my sweat-doused hair, ready to get Chalupa out of jail.

Next time, I hope you do a better job keeping things on the low, Chalupa, because I'm not sure how many more lies the LPPD is going to believe before they start hunting us down one by one.

LACEY

The day started out like normal, sitting at my desk going through an obscene amount of paperwork, holding the pen between my teeth while I scrambled to get everything done in a timely fashion.

I've been a prosecuting attorney for the City of La Playa for such a long time that I sometimes forget how heavily involved I get in every case I take, and I'm certainly one that likes a full catalogue of solved cases rather than letting some slip through the cracks.

Everyone in my life had always told me that I needed to let loose every once in a while, and that I shouldn't let work consume my entire life, but the truth was if I wanted to continue being good at my job, I had no choice. It wasn't often that the cases I took on were free of thrills, and there was usually something new to be discovered at every corner. We had a pretty good dynamic going in the office, and the criminals we prosecuted didn't often get away with their crimes.

I was sitting at my desk when I heard a knock on my

door. It was the ADA himself, slipping in with a cup of hot coffee in his hand, the steam rising up into his face.

"Hello, Lacey," he said.

"Don't you have anything better to do than slip in here to see what I'm up to, Richard?" I asked, and he smiled back at me, making himself comfortable in the chair in front of my desk and staring back at me while I continued to work.

"You've been here late every night, Lacey. You know, some of us get all our work done and still manage to have a social life. You're a catch, and it doesn't make sense that you're not out there dating right now," he teased.

"You and I both know that I'm already romantically involved with my job, and with all the time I spend backlogging cases, I really don't have time to be dating anyone. Or would you rather I let my performance at work suffer for someone to take me out to dinner?" I asked, glaring at him.

"Now, I don't think that it has to be one or the other. You are perfectly capable of handling them both, and I know it's been a while since you've been out on a date, but you need it. Trust me, I see how frustrated you are every day, how exhausted you are when you return to the office the next morning after a long night, and you need a break."

"I don't have time for a break, Richard," I replied, running my fingers through a few folders in the filing cabinet near my desk.

"Think about it, Lacey. What's the point of doing all this great work if you don't have someone to share your successes with? You're a great prosecutor, and you deserve to have a little fun too is all. I want to set you up with someone I think you might like, and it may help take some of the edge off around here." I knew he meant well, but a blind date really wasn't on the cards for me with all the work I still had to get done.

"I don't think so. Not something I'm interested in,

Richard, but I genuinely appreciate the effort." I sipped my coffee and picked up my pen, as if to make my point.

"Suit yourself, Lacey, but the offer stands," he replied, getting up to leave my office.

I knew quite well that he wasn't going to stop teasing me until I put myself out there again, but it was something I was willing to deal with because my heart was in my work.

I couldn't see myself coming home to someone, telling them about how work was, not being able to divulge any of the real details, only to pretend that this job was not absolutely exhausting. I love what I do, but I wasn't ready to share that part of me with anyone, and frankly, I didn't think that love would ever be something I would indulge in. I just didn't have the time for it.

I sighed and sipped my coffee while I continued going through cases. I thought a lot about what Richard said, but I didn't have it in me to go out with this friend of his, especially because Richard knew absolutely nothing about what kind of men I was interested in.

I decided it would be best to call up someone who genuinely understood me and get everything off my chest. I called my best friend, Mona, hoping that she would be able to side with me on this one, because anyone that Richard would've picked for me to go on a date with would probably be just as self-obsessed as he was.

"Hey, Lacey! You're still at the office, what could you possibly be calling me about?" she asked, pretending not to know that this was a regular thing we liked to do.

"It's okay, there's no one around. Richard is trying to set me up with someone, telling me that I needed to take a break every once in a while and put myself back out on the market. Is he crazy? There's no way any work would get done if I spent all my time running after men who had no idea what they wanted and would end up disappointing me anyway," I said, rambling over the phone while she listened attentively before chiming in.

"Richard is right, Lacey. You really are married to your job. It wouldn't hurt to let yourself go every once in a while, and you might even find that you feel a bit more refreshed when you return to work, instead of being so uptight all the time," she said.

"Ouch," I said jokingly.

"I tell you these things because I love you, and I don't want to see you crash and burn," she replied.

"I feel like I'm crashing and burning all the time, Mona. You know that this job is hard, I'm constantly working the cases, and let's not forget that I originally wanted to be a defense attorney, but instead I ended up working for the government," I said, wallowing in my sorrow while she continued to try lifting me up.

"I know, Lacey. You have to remember that you're incredible at your job, and I don't think there's anyone that can do what you can. That fire you have inside of you isn't going anywhere, even if you took a break every once in a while." For the first time I started to warm to the idea.

"I'll think about it," I replied, realizing that she might have a point. "I'll speak to you later. Gotta go, work to do."

Is there really room for balance in a life like this, or am I just kidding myself?

MOVES

I wasn't about to have a guy ride on the back of my bike, so I took my truck to pick up Chalupa. I parked a few blocks away from the station because the last thing I needed was to have it impounded while I was in there. The minute I approached the LPPD building, there was a familiar sense of tension in the air, one I knew all too well. It was like they could all sense me coming from a mile away, either that or they took one look at my appearance and decided I had to be trouble. I popped the collar on my leather jacket and removed my sunglasses before I approached the desk. I could see the woman sitting behind it clutching her fake pearl necklace, staring at the tattoos on my neck.

"Can I help you?" she asked in a voice that was less than friendly.

"I'm here to post bail for a friend of mine," I said, smiling at her kindly, but I could tell that she was rather afraid of me, even while sitting in the middle of the police department.

"Of course," she said, getting ready to help me process everything.

I needed to get Chalupa out of the cell he'd probably

spent the entire night in, replaying the moment he got caught over in his head, trying to figure out how he managed to slip up. We've been running together long enough for him to know the rules, and I had to make sure that this went down without a hitch, so that I wouldn't have to show my face in the police department again for a long time. They'd all had their suspicions about me and other members of the Outlaw Souls, but I was just afraid they actually had damning evidence this time that could undo everything we'd built together. *I'll discuss it with Chalupa once we're safely out of here,* I thought, trying to ignore the fact that every single pair of eyes were glued to me, staring like they'd just witnessed a murder. *If I stick around too long they're probably gonna try to charge me with something.*

I was led to the back area to wait for Chalupa. I could hear his voice down the hallway as he grabbed the few belongings he had on him at the time. I knew this was just the beginning of the road for us when it came to whatever he got pulled in for, but I was determined to make sure that he got out of this unscathed.

"Hey man, I don't know how to thank you," he said the minute he laid eyes on me.

"This is far from over, Chalupa. Let's get you out of here," I said, leading him out to my truck, watching him take in the fresh air, realizing that he was probably just glad to be out of that awful cell.

"I'm going to drive you out to Hacienda, and get to the bottom of what's going on, but I need you to stay out of trouble while I do that. Okay?" I said, and he nodded at me. He looked scared, like he knew that they probably had more to go on than he was letting on, but I couldn't question him until we were well out of earshot of anyone that could use that information against us. It wasn't long before we pulled up outside his home, where he lived with his elderly mother, a sweet woman who had no idea that he was involved with the Outlaw Souls. It was probably best that it stayed that way because it was the perfect place for him to go when something like this happened, and I needed him safe so I could consult with everyone else to figure out what we were going to do.

"What's going to happen if I have to go to jail?"

"That depends on what you did, Chalupa. You need to tell me what they brought you in for in the first place."

"They picked me up when they thought I was the one that stole a car with the intent of chopping it. They must've followed me, gotten me on security footage somewhere. Man, I don't know where they got that information from, but I was out minding my own business and then next thing I know, I was being handcuffed."

"Goddamn it, Chalupa. You have to get better at covering your tracks, man. I don't know how much trouble you're in right now, but we're gonna get you out of this mess. I need you to lay low for a little while. No trying to run any jobs while you're here. You wouldn't want your mother finding out about what you're truly doing out there. You don't wanna break her fragile heart, do you, Chalupa?"

"Not at all. I'll lay low, I promise. Though, Moves, I need to tell you, I didn't steal the car. I don't know what kind of case they're trying to build down at the LPPD, but they got it wrong. I didn't think anyone would believe me," he said.

"This is worse than I thought. If you're being framed then we really have our work cut out for us. Lay low, I'll be in touch soon enough," I said, starting up my bike and taking off before he could say anything else. I worried that this was going to end up being bad for the entire club, because if anyone got close enough, they'd be able to start making connections about who we were and what we were involved in. *I just have to make sure I don't let that happen.*

I didn't understand who could be behind this, wondering what they'd get out of having the Outlaw Souls framed. I thought for a moment that it had to be one of our rival gangs, trying to take us out once and for all, but until I knew more I had to be smart about this. I couldn't let Chalupa walk into another trap, and I had to make sure that everyone had what they needed to protect themselves.

If we really do have a threat on our hands, it's only a matter of time before someone tries to take a swing at one of us again.

LACEY

It felt good to be home again, especially after being in the office late every night for the last few weeks. I sat for a moment, peering over my coffee table at the cases I was working on, wondering if Richard was right about my life. I was so consumed with work that I had forgotten what it was like to let loose and enjoy myself every once in a while. I knew his heart was in the right place, but there was no way I'd ever consider going out with someone that he lined up for me. Judging from the people he spent his downtime with, I knew they wouldn't be the right fit for me.

I truly believed that I didn't have any time for such things, that my life was far too complicated, and I had to stay focused on my career if I wanted to get anywhere. It was the kind of lifestyle that left me exhausted, but utterly fulfilled. I wasn't sure there was a place for romance in my life, but I was starting to warm up to the idea of at least giving it a try.

I ventured off into my small kitchen to put the kettle on the stove for another cup of tea to get me through the next round of paperwork I had to deal with, but right as I filled it up and set it down, I heard a knock on my door. I looked through the peephole to see my next-door neighbors waving, waiting for me to open up the door.

"Hello, Lacey! It's nice to see you home for once!" said Lily, my delightful neighbor. I didn't get to see much of them with my job being so demanding.

"It's nice to see you too, Lily and Bailey. What brings you both around?" I asked.

"Well, we're having a little birthday celebration tonight over at our place, and we'd like for you to join us," Bailey said, with a big, beaming grin on her face. "I know that you've been crazy busy, and to be quite honest I didn't even know if you were going to be home today, but since you are, we'd both love it if you joined us."

"I don't know, I have a lot of work I need to get through, and I don't have nearly enough time," I said, even though I was really contemplating joining them.

"Well, if you change your mind, please don't hesitate to come by. Our door is always open," Lily said, and I smiled at her. It was kind of them to open their door to me, and at that moment, I was trying to convince myself that I needed to focus on work, but then I remembered the conversation I'd had with both Richard and Mona earlier. They both wanted me to branch out, and I was starting to think that it was maybe something I needed to do.

"Thank you both very much," I said, watching them walk away while I shut my front door. I stood behind it for a moment, knowing that it wouldn't hurt to step away from work for the night just to have a little fun. I remember how my mother would tell me that I had no social life, and that going through the motions every day would start to get rather boring if I didn't do something exciting every once in a while. I started rummaging through my closet for something to wear, having absolutely no idea how to dress for the occasion, or any occasion for that matter.

It had been such a long time since I'd worn anything apart from my comfortable blazers and straight-legged pleated pants. I wanted to throw on a pair of jeans, pull my hair back, and get out of my comfort zone for a little while. So I took a hot shower, organized all of the case files on my coffee table before slipping into my outfit of choice. The light-blue denim hugged my hips comfortably while I slipped into a black lace-trimmed camisole. I took one look in the mirror and I truly didn't recognize myself. I couldn't remember the last time I'd dressed up with a place to go, and I couldn't help but bask in the moment.

Evening approached when I finally made it out the door, watching the cars pull up outside of Lily and Bailey's home. For a moment, I staggered back, wondering if I should turn around and head back inside my house because it dawned on me that I didn't know anyone. I barely knew Lily and Bailey as it was, but I knew it wasn't going to be easy meeting all these new people, especially after not having much of a social life for more months than I could count. I decided to swallow my fear, lock my front door, and head over to their house, where I rang the doorbell, and was greeted by a smiling Lily.

"You came! Oh my goodness, I'm so glad," she said as she came in for an embrace. I hugged her back politely while she dragged me inside, and I took in how beautifully decorated her home was. Everything was in its perfect place, with eclectic vases on the bookshelves, different variations of plants lining the windowsills, and sheer curtains that would let a lovely amount of sunlight into each room. It was such a step up from my home, which was a bunch of furniture that I bought in an estate sale because I was too busy to make it to any furniture showrooms. I took whatever I could find, getting the basics down so I could focus on work.

The worry still settled in the back of my mind that I was losing precious time by being here, but I wanted to enjoy myself, and I knew that I would probably be better off if I did so. Everyone had already been laughing, drinking, and enjoying themselves to the fullest when I arrived, but I realized just how much I wanted in on the action. I felt the adrenaline course through me as Bailey came over and handed me a drink in a red Solo cup. I downed the thick liquid that burned into my throat, finishing it with a smile.

"Well, there is certainly more where that came from," Bailey said, taking my empty cup away so she could bring me another even after I told her I was good.

"Would you like something to eat, Lacey? Please, help yourself to whatever you'd like. I want you to meet a few of my friends and my incessant brother," Lily said, shooting a look at one of the guys that was leaning on the fireplace, acknowledging my presence with a little tilt of his head.

"This is Ryder, Bailey and my brother, and that's Paige, our sister," she said, pointing everyone out while they waved back at me.

"Hello, it's nice to meet you all. My name is Lacey," I said, feeling rather intimidated by all of them. They all looked like they had quite the bond, and for a moment I began to wonder what I was really doing there. I couldn't help but notice how nice everyone was, and how great it felt to strike up a conversation or two with them. Paige was the first to fully introduce herself, sitting me down while Bailey brought in another round of drinks, so we could all get to know each other a little better.

"So, tell me, Lacey, what do you do for a living?" Paige asked in between sips of her beer.

"I'm a prosecuting attorney. Sounds much more glamorous than it actually is, trust me," I said, starting to feel the alcohol seep into my veins.

"That's incredible. Quite taxing, isn't it?" she asked, and I nodded, while we all proceeded to get far too drunk. It felt good to have a little buzz, and right as Paige and I were delving into a bit more conversation, I saw Lily at the head of the entryway with a man standing next to her, who she introduced as Scott.

There was something incredibly welcoming about Lily and Bailey's friends, and they were all so kind to me that I was starting to wonder why I even tried getting out of this little celebration in the first place. It was the first time I'd felt comfortable anywhere other than the office in a long time, and I was starting to think that everyone had been right about me. I was too caught up in my job, too lost in all the cases I would work through every day, and I needed a little break.

I'm just glad that I took Lily and Bailey up on their offer, otherwise I probably would've been curled up on my couch all night trying to get some work done, ordering some takeout and heading to bed. That is certainly not the exciting night Richard and Mona both wanted for me, but I'm not sure that this is the place I'm going to find someone I'm interested in.

I sat there for a moment with another drink in my hand, trying to decide if I even knew what my type was. Of all the guys I'd dated in the past, no one had made my heart flutter the way it was supposed to, no one ever challenged me or excited me the way I always wanted. *Maybe I just don't know what I want,* I thought, noticing that Lily had caught the fact that I had zoned out a bit.

"Hey, what's on your mind?" she asked, reading the expression on my face.

"Just trying not to think about work for the night. Pathetic, isn't it?"

"No, it isn't. You work very hard, Lacey. We've barely said two words to each other and I know that. You come home at all hours of the night, looking so exhausted, and I'm just glad that you seem to have perked up a bit while you've been here.

I wanted to invite you over before, but you weren't ever home," she said.

"I live at the office more than I do in my own house, but I'm starting to think that has to change," I said, opening up to her.

"It's never too late to make that change, Lacey. Sometimes you just need a little excitement in your life." I completely agreed with Lily on that one.

About an hour passed before asked Lily where her bathroom was. She pointed upstairs and to the first door on the left, and I headed up, struggling to keep my footing steady with all the alcohol that was coursing through my system. When I finally got to the top of the stairs, I began making my way to the bathroom door when I bumped into someone. My eyes were glued to his feet until I looked up at his face. I lurched back and he held me by the shoulders, keeping me from falling.

"Are you okay?" he asked, his voice warm and comforting.

"I'm sorry. I was just looking for the bathroom," I said, trying not to make eye contact with him because he was far too handsome for me to be having a conversation with as drunk as I was. I looked down at the tattoos on his arm, wondering what their stories were, because they were rather unique. I was a bit fixated on them when he finally stepped aside so I could pass, smiling and chuckling to himself.

"I don't think we've met. My name is Michael, but everyone calls me Moves," he said, and I smiled back at him.

"Now that is quite the nickname. My name is Lacey, I'm Lily and Bailey's neighbor and they invited me over to celebrate their birthday, but I am really drunk. I'm probably not making much sense right now," I said, giggling.

"No, no. You're making perfect sense, Lacey. It's nice to meet you. Now, I know you were heading for the bathroom, but please be careful on your way out because you nearly fell right back down the stairs," he said, snickering.

"I will, thank you, Michael. Uh, Moves," I said, getting into the bathroom and slamming the door behind me while I tried to distance myself from the awkwardness of that last encounter.

I don't know what came over me. I'm not usually like this. Man, has my tolerance really gone down this much? Sitting there, head in hands, I tried to take stock of the situation.

I stood at the wash basin washing my hands and staring at my reflection in the mirror while I tried to sober up a bit before heading back out. I ran my fingers through my hair, calming myself down. I opened the door to find Moves still waiting at the head of the stairs for me.

"You're still here?"

"I just wanted to make sure you didn't tumble headfirst and give yourself a concussion," he said, and I smiled.

"You're very kind," I said as he outstretched his hand, motioning for me to head down the stairs behind him. I felt my cheeks get hot, and I knew I had to be blushing under the warm low lighting above the staircase. Once we made it to the bottom, we were met by both Lily and Bailey saying goodbye to a few of their friends.

"Where were you two?" Lily asked teasingly.

"Moves was just helping me find the bathroom," I said, and she laughed.

"Thank you for that," she said, addressing him.

"Lily, Bailey, I just want to thank you for getting me to come out tonight. Trust me, I really needed it. I'm going to be heading out now," I said, looking over at Moves, who seemed rather concerned that I was going to walk in my condition.

"Please, I'll come with you, drop you off at your door," he said, leading me out.

"Have a lovely evening, Lacey. Thank you for coming!" Lily shouted while Moves led me back home to my front door, and I fumbled around for my keys to let myself in.

"Thank you again, Moves, for walking me home. I have to say that I'm not usually like this, and apparently I've become somewhat of a lightweight after all this time," I said, and he grinned.

"It's no problem, Lacey. I hope you have a nice evening." He let me head inside and then waved goodbye before taking off. I collapsed onto the couch, basking in the moment of meeting an extraordinarily handsome man, who I'd probably never be able to face again because he'd certainly seen me at my worst.

I thought about how willing he was to come to my rescue, and how nice he had been to me after we had just met. I lay there, outstretching my legs on the couch, realizing that this was probably the first time I'd ever felt a spark between me and another person. I felt my stomach flutter and my cheeks flush, and it was then that I began to see that there may have been a bit of chemistry between us. *It doesn't matter, though, because I doubt I'll ever be seeing him again.* There was something about him, though, that I couldn't quite fathom.

MOVES

I was overseeing weapons shipments in the warehouse, making sure we weren't missing any key pieces of inventory when I heard my phone buzz. I looked down at the number to see that it was Ryder, and I could feel it in my gut that he had news about what was happening to Chalupa. I answered, waiting for him to give me whatever information he could.

"Ryder."

"Hey, Moves. I need to talk to you about Chalupa getting picked up by the LPPD. He's probably already told you that he had nothing to do with that stolen car, and if he did we would definitely know about it. It's all bullshit, man, and I think I know why." My heart started beating in my chest at the thought of what could be causing all of this.

"What's that, Ryder?"

"I think someone is trying to frame Ortega's Autos as a chop shop." There was an element of anger and urgency in Ryder's voice. "Whoever is doing this has to have had enough inside information to lead the police down there. We need to find out what's going on before another one of our own is picked up."

"I'm working on it," I said. "I think I can convince Hawk to help me get to the bottom of this. I should probably let you know ahead of time that Chalupa doesn't have enough money on his own to hire a good attorney for his defense, so we're all gonna vote on taking some club funds to get the job done."

"We protect our own," Ryder agreed.

"Yes, we do. Chalupa is going to be just fine as long as we're able to keep him from going to jail. Hey, Ryder, do you think we're dealing with a rival gang situation here? Do you think they're trying to get the police on our tail so they could take us out for good?" I asked, wanting to hear his opinion before I jumped into an investigation.

"I think it's definitely possible, but something seems different this time. It feels a lot more personal than I'd like to admit, but I'm keeping an eye out for any suspicious activity and I suggest you do the same," he said.

"Be careful out there. I'll get in touch if Hawk and I find anything," I said before hanging up.

I sighed, trying to decide how best to go about this because we couldn't risk getting the police back on our tail again. If they managed to get an inside look at our operations, it would only be a matter of time before everything we'd ever built came crumbling down.

I worried about Chalupa, about what was going to happen if we got him the right attorney but he still went to jail anyway. I knew very well how these things worked, and there was no telling whether the odds were really in our favor or not. I still needed to find out what kind of evidence they had on Chalupa to even arrest him in the first place, especially because he never so much as got near the car they'd supposedly picked him up for.

I thought for a moment about the possibility of someone tipping off the cops, getting them to take any course of action to infiltrate the Outlaw Souls on a hunch, and every thought only made me angrier. We'd already done so much to protect ourselves and this threat seemed to come at a time when we were still trying to find our footing again. I certainly was, and it was still a struggle every day to get up and remember that I had responsibilities to the Outlaw Souls. I couldn't take a step back, not when everyone needed me. Now, Chalupa needed me, and I had to find a way to get him out of this mess.

I remembered overhearing at the party last night that the girl Lily and Bailey invited over was a prosecuting attorney. She'd seemed nice, and certainly wasn't what I was expecting for that job title, but I had to believe that she was a different woman when she was at work. I wondered if she'd be able to shed some light on a good attorney for Chalupa—that is, if she wasn't involved with all of this herself.

I did think it was quite strange that she was the only one among us that wasn't part of the Outlaw Souls, or directly related to it. She was the only stranger in our den, and while it could just be that Lily and Bailey wanted to extend a polite invitation, there was something strange about that girl. Something that gave me a gut feeling that I'd probably see her again.

I have to focus. If what Ryder said is true, and that someone is trying to frame Ortega's as a chop shop, then I don't have very much time to figure out what's going on. I need to call Hawk, and we need to start our search as quickly as possible.

I pulled out my phone again to give him a call, so we could finally discuss what we were going to do about our threat, all while trying to protect one of our own from facing any jail time.

I knew Chalupa was scared, and I knew the news of all of this had left everyone confused, but I was determined to put an end to these threats so we could go back to living our lives with a sense of normality. We were all left at a standstill, trying to make the best of a terrible situation, but we had to have each other's backs.

We have no choice but to pull through for him.

LACEY

My head was splitting with the most excruciating headache, and I truly felt like I was back in college again. I didn't even know how I'd managed to drag myself back to work, but there I was mulling over my lukewarm coffee trying to focus on the paperwork I needed to get done. My mind kept going back to the night prior, to how much fun I'd had, and all the amazing people I'd met. Part of me felt fulfilled that I'd managed to step outside of my comfort zone, but the other part felt stressed and frustrated that I'd let the work pile up.

I felt a familiar flutter in my stomach every time I thought of the man I'd met, who had a nickname I'd never heard before. *Moves, huh?* I thought, completely drowning out any sounds in the office around me, but it wasn't long before I had one of the receptionists hovering over my desk trying to get my attention.

"Lacey? Lacey?"

I snapped out of my daydream. Nobody had seen me with a hangover before. No wonder she sounded a little concerned.

"Yes, sorry. What is it?"

"The DA would like to see you in his office," she said. For

a moment I wondered if Richard had managed to convince the DA that I needed some time off as well. I shook the ridiculous thought from my mind, straightening my blazer before heading into his office, where he promptly motioned for me to sit.

"Good morning, Lacey. Please, there's something we need to discuss," he said sternly. I gulped, trying to keep a straight face while he fumbled through a few of the papers on his desk before looking up at me.

"Sir, may I ask what this is about?"

"We've received word that there's a chop shop over in North La Playa that needs taking down, but we don't have nearly enough evidence to do so. I'm putting you on the case, and I'm going to need you to do a little research off the books if we plan on nailing these guys," he said, and I knew exactly what that meant.

"You want me to go undercover?" I asked, not sure if I was understanding him correctly.

"That's correct, Lacey. You're the only one that has their head on straight around here, and I think you'd be right for the job. I know everyone gives you a hard time about how much of your life you spend in the office, but consider this opportunity a pat on the back for a job well done," he said, and it was probably the first time he'd ever personally acknowledged any of the work I'd done.

"Where would you like me to begin?" I asked, trying to swallow the fact that I was absolutely terrified. I didn't know the first thing about making a good impression on people, especially when it came to hiding what my true purpose was. I had to give myself some credit, because my lawyer instincts were certainly going to come in handy when it came to getting under each and every suspect's skin. I thought this could be my moment to make a name for myself and actually feel like I'd accomplished something real for a change.

"We've already arrested one guy that has some connections to that place, and it's going to be enough to get you the information you need to start scoping the place out. If we plan on making additional arrests, we have to make sure that we have enough to shut the shop down for good. I feel like it has been in operation for quite some time and I refuse to let this go on any longer. I'm going to give you this file, which has everything you need to know about the interrogation we conducted on the first guy we arrested. Have a look over it and figure out how you're going to get close enough to find out more. These people can smell cops coming from a mile away, and I have a feeling they'd never be able to tell with you, Lacey. Make me proud, and I will make this worth your while," he said, and I nodded.

"Thank you, sir." I left his office clutching the file he'd given me to my chest while I made the walk back to my office to figure out what my first move was going to be. Richard caught up with me for a moment before I managed to close the door, smiling, as though he'd learned what I had been up to the night prior.

"You look incredibly happy. I wonder why that might be," he said, fishing for information, but it was quite clear that he didn't know anything.

"I just received the biggest case of my career, and now I'm going to go off into my office, read the file, and get to work. No more pressing me about guys, but if you must know, I met someone last night that did pique my interest for a little while." I felt my cheeks heat up again, but I was enjoying teasing Richard for a change.

"Is that so? So that's why you look like hell today. Rough night out drinking, huh?"

"It was my neighbor's birthday, nothing too wild. I promise to tell you more once I get through this case, all right?"

"Counting on it," he said, shutting my office door behind him. I sat there for a moment, reading everything that the suspect had said, noticing how many considerable loopholes there were in his story. So much of what he said didn't make sense no matter what context it was used in. It was like he was desperately trying to cover his tracks.

There's something strange going on at that place, and I'm just going to have to figure out what that is.

MOVES

I was up extra early that morning, sitting in my small kitchen, downing a cup of hot coffee as I thought about where the day was going to take me. I'd checked in with Chalupa the night before, making sure that he was doing all right and lying low while we got to the bottom of all of this. I knew that he was scared, that he had no idea who could've done this to him.

Hawk and I were still trying to figure out how best to go about looking around for any clues, but we had to stay out of sight because any indication that we were anywhere near the scene and we'd probably be picked up as well.

It was driving me insane not knowing who could be next, worried for each member of the Outlaw Souls, wondering what would happen if any of them got caught out at the wrong place at the wrong time. I made sure to schedule the meeting with all of them down at the Blue Dog, because they all needed to know exactly what they were looking out for and who to avoid while we got to work on finding out who was trying to frame Ortega's.

I thought about the possibilities, about Las Balas, the rival gang that did the really nasty stuff that we wouldn't touch. Were they trying to run us out of town so they could take over? I wasn't going to let that happen. I was going to make sure that everyone had access to the right weapons, that we accounted for every single gun and dollar that traveled in and out of the Outlaw Souls. I was so afraid that something was going to get leaked, that we were going to be at our most vulnerable if they were ever able to get inside information from one of our own. I had to trust the other members, because as the enforcer, I had to make sure that no one slipped up while we were under such scrutiny.

I went outside into the yard to give my bike a tune-up, checking for my gun in its holster at my back before I rode down to the Blue Dog, feeling the collar of my leather jacket brush against my neck in the wind.

The heat was scorching when I finally arrived, and I felt a single drop of sweat trickle down my forehead as I entered the Blue Dog. I saw all the familiar faces I'd been waiting to see since Chalupa got arrested, and I could tell by the concern in their expressions that they were waiting for the answers we simply didn't have. I wished I could've told them that I had everything figured out, that I wasn't right there with them wondering who could've tipped off the police, because until we had solid evidence, we couldn't even be sure that it was Las Balas.

"It's about time, Moves," Ryder said, giving me the side-eye as though he was expecting me to be here and ready to talk before everyone else arrived.

"I'm sorry I'm late, everyone. As you know, we have a bit of a situation on our hands. You all know what happened to Chalupa, and how he ended up at the police station with charges relating to stealing a car with the intention of getting it chopped, even though he was nowhere near the vehicle in question," I explained.

"How can you be so sure?" Ryder asked again, looking

around the room for support while everyone stood back in silence.

"I'm sure because I saw the look in his eyes when he told me he had nothing to do with it. You were the one that told me this entire thing was bullshit to begin with, and now you're having doubts? We're all in this together because we trust each other, because we protect our own, and it's time that we start doing that. This is a threat to the Outlaw Souls, one that could very well destroy us if we're not careful," I replied.

"I said that because I believed it was Las Balas. They're the only ones that would have reason to mess with us, and it would be good for them having one of our own go to jail. Can you imagine what they would do with La Playa if we were run out of town?"

"They would turn our town into a drug ring, and I want no part in it," I said, raising my hand. "Neither should any of you. Now that we have that settled, you should all know that Hawk and I will be investigating this further, trying to get some solid evidence before we go around accusing people, even if we feel like we have reason to do so. The real reason I asked you all to be here today is because Chalupa is going to need a good attorney if he's going to get out of this, and he doesn't have the cash to pay out of pocket on his own. I would like to raise a vote to take some of the club funds to help him out."

"We don't have a lot of funds as it is," Scorpion said, and I nodded.

"We protect our own," I reminded them, and I watched the remaining hands rise.

"Then it's settled. We're going to get Chalupa the representation he needs, and we're going to bring him home."

I stood around there watching everyone cheer, realizing that over the course of a few years, we'd really built a family here together, one that Padre would've been proud to see in action today. I thought for a moment about what Chalupa had said the day he got arrested, telling me that I should've never even thought about giving up my name because of how significant it was. Being here with all of them reminded me that I was still a part of that family, even though we'd lost one of our own, and I had to make sure that didn't happen again.

We're going to get you out, Chalupa.

LACEY

I don't know the first thing about undercover work, and I'm scared they're going to see right through me the moment I pull up there pretending to be someone I'm not. I have no idea who these people are, how dangerous they could possibly be, or what's really going on, but I'd be lying if I said I wasn't curious. I have to keep a straight face and pretend to be naïve. If they start to catch on that I'm investigating them, and something is indeed wrong here, I don't know how long I'm actually going to last.

Yes, I was scared, but this was a job given to me directly from the DA himself and I couldn't disappoint. They saw an opportunity to get to the bottom of what was happening at Ortega's Autos, and if it would mean putting some criminals behind bars, then I had to do my part in assisting.

I glanced at my reflection in the entryway mirror, pulling my hair back into a low ponytail while I took a deep breath, trying to relax my face and get rid of the fear that sat conspicuously behind my eyes. I gathered my thoughts, remembering why I'd agreed to do this in the first place, and headed out into the parking lot to have a look at my car.

I pulled out my cell phone, doing a quick search for

potential car problems that I could inflict myself with in order to have a good excuse for showing up at Ortega's. I decided on one that I could get done under the hood of the car itself, and hoping that it wouldn't break down before I got there, I popped the hood, fiddled around with parts I didn't even know existed until I felt something finally loosen up, and dropped it shut.

I got into the driver's seat and wound down the front windows for some air, but it didn't help much with the scorching heat and beaming sun overhead. I threw on a pair of sunglasses, started the engine, and took off down the road, making my way to Ortega's, ready to get to the bottom of what was really going on there.

When I pulled up in front of the place, my heart was beating so loudly that I swore I heard it in my ears, but I tried not to panic, watching the hood of my car begin to smoke, while a man approached me from outside.

"Whoa, what seems to be the problem?" the guy asked, and I got out of the car, shaking my head, pretending like I didn't know exactly what I'd done to get it in that condition.

"We're a little short-staffed today, but I'm sure I can give it a quick look," he said, and I nodded.

"That would be amazing." I said, and he smiled. "I don't know what happened to it, but I have somewhere to be in a few hours, and I'm afraid I'm not going to get very far without my car. I really appreciate you taking the time to help." I glanced down at his tattoos, the sweat rim around his neck on his white wifebeater, while he grabbed the rag in his pocket to wipe his hands.

"Come on inside, it's way too hot out here," he said, and I smiled, heading into the open garage while he reached into the mini fridge at the side, offering me a bottle of water.

"Thank you very much," I said, taking it from him, opening it up, and taking my first sip while I glanced around the garage for anything suspicious. It all looked like a normal, functional garage, and there wasn't any sign of carmachines being disassembled, but then again, I had no idea what was happening around back. What I saw on the surface looked pretty normal to me, but I started to have a bad feeling, like I was missing something that was right under my nose. I began to walk around, while the nice man brought my car in and started looking under the hood. I eyed the toolboxes, the benches, the wires that tangled on the floor, while I looked down to watch where I was going.

I don't see anything here that would give me reason to believe this place is a chop shop, but maybe I'm not looking hard enough.

I heard the man call out for me to come and join him, and I was sure he'd found the root of the problem, which was of course, my handiwork.

"How in the world did you manage to do this?" he asked, and I shrugged my shoulders.

"I have absolutely no idea. I ran out of my front door a few hours ago in a rush, but I noticed that there was something weird with the ignition when I started it up. Is it fixable? Or is it going to cost me an arm and a leg?" I asked, acting like I was really worried.

"It's nothing too severe. I can have it done in an hour or so, if you'd be okay with waiting around," he said, and I smiled.

"Of course." I sat down on the white plastic chair that was directly under the shade of the garage door while I watched him work. I finished my water in the scorching heat, feeling the sweat start to trickle down the back of my neck, and I wished I would've worn something a bit cooler to venture all the way out here.

I sat while he worked on my car, trying to take in my surroundings and keep an eye out for any suspicious activity. A few people came and went, but other than the occasional appreciative glance, nobody paid me much attention, for which I was grateful. A delivery van showed up with what I presumed were spare parts, and someone came out of an office to sign for them. There was a radio playing in the back and I could hear a man singing along as he worked.

The time seemed to pass rather quickly, and before I knew it he was finishing up the job. I thanked him and paid him for his services, got in my car, and drove away, without seeing any kind of sign of any strange behavior coming from anyone that was working in the shop. I remembered the faces I saw today, just in case I would have to deal with them again, but nothing struck me as odd.

I'm terrible at this. I need to do better, I thought, feeling my stomach grumble. I passed a small restaurant named Tiny's and decided to turn around and head back there for a bite to eat.

I headed inside and was greeted by one of the waitresses that was scooting by with a large tray stacked with plates of food.

"Sit anywhere you like, hun," she said in a high pitched, nasally voice, and I thanked her. I took a small table that was out of the way but had a good view of the place. Peering over the menu while I decided what to eat, I looked around to see if anyone looked suspicious. *I really suck at this detective stuff,* I thought. Everybody looked perfectly normal to me; if there were any criminals lurking around, I certainly couldn't tell.

When the waitress returned, I ordered a burger and fries and poured a glass of water from the pitcher she brought, just as I heard the whirring of bike engines coming from right outside the restaurant.

I looked up at the door to see a few bikers trail in with their matching leather jackets and menacing expressions, behaving like they owned the place. I watched as they took the booth at the far end of the room, trying to stay out of sight, but something about them made me feel uneasy. I wasn't one to judge, but I'd heard about the biker that had recently been arrested for stealing a car, and the suspect that was arrested after him, both supposedly with ties to Ortega's Autos. I was starting to wonder whether these bikers had anything to do with what was really going on at the auto shop, but I needed to do more digging to find out for myself.

They sat down in a booth right near the bathroom, but I couldn't get a close enough look at them to see their faces, in case they come around the next time I was visiting Ortega's for more clues.

I finished up my meal as quickly as I could, rolling the heel of my shoe while I tried to convince myself that I was making the right decision, but I had to make a move. I stood up to leave, throwing enough cash on the table to cover the bill, and headed to the back where the bikers were huddled over their menus. I played the part expertly, rolling my heel again, tripping just enough to grab ahold of their table, startling them.

"Oh my God, I'm so sorry. This stupid shoe," I said, tucking the loose strands of my hair behind my ear while they all looked up at me and smiled. The man sitting directly across from where I stood nodded at me kindly.

"It's not a problem at all," he said, and I walked off into the bathroom, making sure I remembered each and every one of their faces.

I turned on the tap, trying to waste some time before heading back out, but for some reason, my heart was pounding in my chest. I couldn't understand why, and I couldn't put the feeling in the pit of my stomach into words, but I had a bad feeling that they were connected to all of this somehow.

Get yourself together, Lacey. You have to see this through, no matter what it takes. This is your job. If the DA thinks you can pull this off, then you're going to have to get a whole lot better at playing the part.

I dried my hands and left, smiling at them as I passed and headed out into the scorching heat to get back into my car and return to the office.

I hated that I was going to show up without a sliver of evidence or anything pointing to any criminal activity happening anywhere near Ortega's Autos, but I knew I still had a lot of digging to do if I was going to be sure. As I drove back, I started plotting my next move, debating how I was going to get close enough to start asking questions without anyone suspecting me. I had a feeling I would be seeing a lot more of those bikers the next time I headed back to Ortega's, and I knew I had to play this smart.

Don't let them catch on. You have to play the part.

MOVES

I needed to clear my head, so I decided to take a solo ride out to Vegas to blow off a little steam and start thinking about how we were going to take care of the situation at hand without getting anyone else hurt. I could feel the fear settle into my bones, the worry that we were about to face something much bigger than just a petty theft, and I wasn't going to stand by and watch the Outlaw Souls get taken out.

I promised myself that once things were settled with Chalupa, I was going to make sure Hawk and I had the time we needed to start looking into what really happened the day Chalupa got picked up. I truly believed that there had to be a slip-up somewhere, a clue that would point us in the right direction of the person responsible for trying to get the police on our tail. The drive gave me the time I needed to think, to reminisce about how far we'd all come since Padre had died.

I realized that I was going to have to start thinking about other options when it came to finding an attorney that would be willing to represent Chalupa, especially knowing the reputation we had around La Playa.

I'd been estranged from my family for years, barely even remembering a family other than the Outlaw Souls, because over time, I tried my best to block out the memories and the pain that came with it all. I knew that I would have to face them all at some point, and now I was starting to think it was time I got in touch with my brother, who was working as a criminal defense attorney. I could only hope that he would be willing to help.

I knew I was going to have to live through the spiel of him telling me that I should've stayed in touch, that I should've been a better brother, but I'd tried my best to leave that part of my life behind and move on to better things. I found a home and people to care about when I joined the Outlaw Souls, and I never had any reason to look back. However, now one of our own was in trouble, and I truly believed that my brother could point me in the right direction of someone who would be willing to represent Chalupa.

I hated how I felt whenever the memories of my past life came flooding back in, remembering what it was like to be raised in an abusive home alongside my brother, Keith. It was the kind of pain that would stick with me for the rest of my life, making sure that I never acted that way out of anger or duress, no matter how tempting it might be to give in to that anger. I thought about how scared we had been as boys, how hard it was for us both to get away from that life and look to a brighter future.

I wasn't even sure that Keith was going to talk to me, but I had no choice other than to find out for myself. I was surprised that he was still hanging around Vegas, but I supposed that was where he had built a home for himself, as I had in La Playa. I worried that he wasn't going to want to hear me out, brushing me off the same way I did to him when I decided to leave all of it behind, but I had to convince him that it was something important. He had an inkling of what

I'd been up to, but I tried to keep the details to a minimum because I knew where he stood with the law, and it only made things more complicated between us.

I arrived at his home, or the place where I'd last seen him, and got off my bike, taking a deep breath before walking up the few steps to ring the doorbell. I watched the door open behind the screen, and there he was, looking older and more exhausted than when I'd seen him last, but he didn't seem too happy to see me. I wouldn't have been surprised if he decided to slam the door in my face for how I'd behaved last time we spoke, but instead, I watched his eyes soften, realizing that he could already tell that I was there on business.

He came out into the front yard with me, and I heard the soft murmurs of who I believed to be his family as he shut the door. I already felt like he didn't want me there, but to see him doing so well for himself, knowing that he didn't need me anymore, made me feel a little hurt, even if I didn't want it to. We stood there in silence for a moment.

"What are you doing here, Michael?"

"I didn't mean to drop in here unannounced, Keith, but I need help." I could tell that he was trying to read the expression on my face to see how bad it really was.

"I don't know why you would need my help when you have an entire army of bikers at your disposal." I didn't take it to heart, because I felt like I deserved it after the way I treated him.

"It's not something they can help with, Keith. One of them has gotten into some trouble with the law and he needs representation. I'm here to ask if you can point me in the direction of someone who could help." I could tell that he wasn't having any of it.

"Criminals go to jail for their crimes, Michael. That's just the way it is, and whatever your little biker friend did to get picked up by the police, I'm sure he deserves it," said Keith.

"He doesn't deserve it, Keith because he didn't do anything. He's being wrongfully accused. I never would've come here if I thought that Chalupa was guilty. Please, Keith, I'm begging you. I'm running out of options, and if I don't get him representation soon, then the LPPD are going to be sending an innocent man to prison. I know even you wouldn't want something like that."

"Fine. I'm going to give you the name of a guy I know in La Playa. Tell him I sent you and he'll get you the help you need. You better be telling the truth, Michael. I can't take any more lies."

"It's the truth, brother. He needs help, and I promised that I was going to get him out of this mess."

"You should be in good hands, Michael." I knew he was trying to get me to leave before his family had a chance to ask any questions, but I couldn't help but feel guilty for letting our relationship get as bad as it was.

I wondered if there was ever going to be a time when we reconnected, when we would be able to get past the trauma we'd both experienced as children, and finally be able to live as brothers once more. I knew that was probably wishful thinking, especially seeing as how involved he was with his job, how much he valued the justice system, and my involvement with the Outlaw Souls.

I left there with the name and number of the man I was supposed to contact, hoping that he was going to be exactly what Chalupa needed to get out of this mess, so we could focus on what really mattered.

Once you're safe at home, Chalupa, we can finally focus on planning our move against whoever had the audacity to try to mess with us. That's the kind of justice we're going after. It shouldn't be long now.

LACEY

Where do I go from here?

Staring at the clock in my office on Friday afternoon, after having had a conversation with the DA about how little evidence I had been able to gather, I began to plan my next move.

He was pushing me to dig deeper, to befriend some of the people in the area hoping that they would talk. I'd heard a lot about the Blue Dog saloon, and from what I was able to gather, it was the stomping ground of a particular biker gang that would probably be able to point me in the direction of someone that would do enough talking to give me the information I needed.

I headed home, bidding goodbye to Richard on the way out. He'd been avoiding me since he heard that I was given undercover work to do, and I could sense a bit of jealousy in his eyes, but he decided not to pry too much.

Back home, I started rummaging through my closet, looking for something appropriate to wear to a biker bar, but I had no idea what would fit the occasion. I knew that this could go horribly wrong for me if any of them discovered my involvement with the law. I needed to fit in, but I also needed someone who was going to help me let loose and have a bit of fun. It was the only way that I was going to get the attention of any of the biker gang, and so I decided to give my best friend a call to see if she was up for a late-night undercover outing.

"Please tell me you don't have any plans tonight," I asked the moment I heard the phone connect.

"You're in luck, Lacey," Mona replied without hesitation. "I am absolutely free tonight, and judging from the tone of your voice, you have something incredibly exciting in mind."

"I'm not too sure about exciting. The word I'd use would probably be dangerous." I didn't want to give too much away, but it was only fair that Mona knew what she was letting herself in for. "As you know, I've been picking up a bit of extra work at the office and was asked to check out what's been happening at an auto shop in the heart of the city. Apparently, a few bikers were arrested in connection with some illegal operation going on down there, and now I'm walking directly into a biker bar to play dumb and hope that someone tells me what I want to know."

"It sounds like you need someone to get drunk with at this dangerous biker bar. What time are we heading out?" Mona was always up for a bit of excitement, but for me, this was work.

"First of all, this is business only. We have to look like we're having a good time so one of them will talk to us, and I can get a bit of information about what really goes down at a place like that."

"Yes, ma'am," she mocked, laughing as she did.

"I have no idea what to wear, though. Do you think you could help me pick something?"

She laughed again. "I'll be right over."

Mona and I spent the next hour deciding on a perfect

outfit. When we finally settled on one, Mona tried to convince me it looked absolutely sexy, but I felt incredibly uncomfortable and exposed. It wasn't the kind of thing I liked to wear out, but my main goal was trying to get the attention of a few bikers, and Mona insisted that was the way to go.

I followed her advice, hoping that she was going to help me leave my inhibitions at the door when we finally arrived, because the more tense I felt, the more I worried that they were going to figure out what I was doing.

We arrived at the place, and I watched Mona walk ahead of me while I stood back to take in the surroundings. It was loud, there were people at every corner drinking themselves sick, and I could feel the heat emanating from each of their bodies, making it hot and hard to breathe. Mona grabbed ahold of my hand, guiding me through the crowd and finding us a seat at the bar, where she ordered me a drink that sounded like something I'd find at a hardware store.

"I haven't been out like this since college, and I haven't dated at all since law school," I shouted above the noise. "I don't know why I was even given this opportunity. I obviously don't fit in at a place like this."

She gave me a stern look. "Will you relax and enjoy the night, please? I know this may all feel like work right now, but in order to get close to the people you want to rattle for answers, you're going to have to start showing them that you do belong."

The bartender brought over our drinks and I downed mine without thinking, feeling the alcohol burn into my throat. I immediately started to feel tipsy, and it took a few more hits before I was finally starting to loosen up, but I was glad. I was able to let go of my worry, hold on to my sobriety enough to focus on what I had to do, and try to get near someone that would find me attractive enough to hold a conversation.

"So what kind of man are you looking for tonight?" Mona teased.

"Come on, Mona. You know these aren't my type. I like professionals, fairly wealthy, and well-read men." I nudged her because she knew that about me.

"You mean you like boring men, who have boring conversations with you, and take you home to have boring sex."

"Sex is overrated." I rolled my eyes and looked over at her, watching her mouth drop at my words.

"You've got to be kidding me," she said, but just before I had the chance to answer her, a gang of bikers walked in, and everyone turned to look at them. They all greeted each other, shaking hands, laughing, until they caught sight of Mona and me. Some of them were faces I had seen at Tiny's when I was having lunch after my failed attempt at scoping out Ortega's Autos.

One of the men came up to me, smiling, while everyone around him went quiet. I didn't think we stood out that much, but apparently I was wrong. I felt naked sitting there while everyone watched, and I started to worry that maybe it had been a mistake to come after all.

"I don't believe I've seen you here before, darlin'," he said, and I felt even more uncomfortable hearing those words leave his mouth.

"Just looking for a little adventure. Decided to stop in for a drink with my friend here. I hope that's all right," I said, pretending to act tough, even though my heart was pounding loudly in my chest.

"Nothing wrong with that. You two ladies have a nice night." He raised his eyebrow while someone whispered something to him. I began to worry that we'd been found out, but they all walked off, and everyone resumed their conversations.

"What the hell was that about?" asked Mona.

"It seems that this place runs in much smaller circles than I originally thought. I don't know if we're aware of what we're dealing with here, but whatever you do, Mona, please be careful. I don't know how I'm going to get any of them to talk to me."

"You just have to join the party, Lacey. Have a little fun, get a little drunk, and it won't be long before a handsome sexy biker is fawning all over you." She held up her hand to get the barman's attention. "Two more shots when you're ready."

We downed the shots and Mona told me she needed the bathroom. I watched her head across the room, squeezing between two bikers, who engaged her in conversation. One was obviously checking her out. For Mona it seemed so easy. I wasn't that confident—I was just scared something was going to go wrong, that I would be found out, and despite the alcohol, I found it hard to relax.

As soon as Mona returned I decided this was my time. I had to make a move, so I told her to watch our seats while I went to the bathroom. That would give me the space to think, compose myself, and make something happen.

I didn't know what I was thinking, or if this was even going to work, but I knew I had to try if I wanted more information. Just as I exited the bathroom, I glanced over at the door to see a familiar face walk in. Our eyes locked for a moment, and I took in his leather jacket, the tattoos peeking through his shirt, and then I remembered where I had seen them before. *Is that Moves?*

MOVES

I needed a night off from all of this. After talking to my brother, I didn't really feel like doing anything apart from drowning my feelings and hoping some of this would start to sort itself out.

I couldn't help but be overwhelmed after my little visit to Keith's, because he was a walking reminder of the family I had lost, and even though I had gained a new one, it didn't take away the pain I felt inside. I entered the Blue Dog with the intention of drinking myself stupid, hoping that for one night I didn't have to be on high alert, that I could enjoy a few drinks and take my mind off of everything that was stressing me out.

I entered, locking eyes with a woman that I had seen before, and for a moment I was trying to remember where I knew her from, while she held my gaze. *Ah, Lacey,* I thought, remembering her from Lily and Bailey's. I wondered what she was doing in a place like this. I watched her walk back over to her friend after shooting me a smile, and I felt the urge to go over and talk to her.

I was staring for quite a while before Ryder started to approach me, and I knew I had to snap out of the little fantasy I was having and join some of the Outlaw Souls for a few drinks.

"Hey, Moves. Come, sit. Have a few drinks, because you look like hell," he said, and I chuckled.

"I'm going to need something very strong to get my mind off of everything that's going on," I agreed.

He handed me a glass of whiskey, which I downed without blinking. Another one swiftly followed.

"I see you were checking out the beautiful girl over there," Ryder said.

"Lacey," I told him. "I met her at a party, but I still can't figure out what she's doing here. She's got company tonight, but she's not half the looker Lacey is."

I felt the need to go right over to her, flirt with her, and let her know that I found her incredibly attractive. I wasn't sure if it was the alcohol that was coursing through me, or just trying to get away from all the stress I'd been feeling, but I was getting a hard-on at the thought of what I might do to her.

I glanced over at her a couple of times from behind my glass, taking in how absolutely stunning she was, and I was holding myself back from heading over there when I knew I was probably going to say something stupid. I made up my mind right then that I wanted her, and I had a feeling that she might've felt the same way. I put my glass down, heading over to her, and she pretended not to see me when I finally approached.

"Now, this is not a face I expected to see here tonight," I said, and she smiled.

"Like I told your friends over there, Mona and I just wanted to come out, have a little fun. I didn't know that the circles were so tight-knit around here, otherwise I probably would've chosen a different spot," she said with that familiar glimmer in her eyes, the same one that I had seen the night we met.

"You are certainly welcome anytime, Lacey. I'm surprised that you would even be in this part of town."

"Where I come from, there just isn't a place like this," she said, smiling at me, while I sat down next to her. Her friend was starting to take the hint, but she didn't go very far, and I was happy to see that Lacey had such protective people on her side.

A girl that beautiful needs someone around to protect her.

The more I looked at her, the more I found myself wanting to get to know her, to kiss her. We sat there having a rather normal conversation, but my eyes averted to her lips, focusing on the way she spoke, how beautiful her smile was, and I could see her cheeks start to blush.

I remembered the way she'd been stumbling around at Lily and Bailey's house, looking for the bathroom, nearly falling down the stairs. That wasn't what I was seeing this time, because I could feel the tension between us grow, and I thought my mind was playing tricks on me watching her eyes start to glance down at my lips.

We were just about to move on to do something that I'd been wanting to do from the time I'd laid eyes on her, but she quickly broke the conversation, trying to sober us both up, and it was probably for the best. I was trying to snap out of it, but I couldn't help but take in how captivating she was, and I was hanging off every word she said, fighting the urge to bring her close and kiss her.

I didn't quite understand the feeling that had overtaken me, and for the first time in a while, I wasn't caught up in worrying about all of my responsibilities. I finally had the opportunity to let loose and enjoy myself without my pain creeping back in reminding me that I needed to stay focused, otherwise I could potentially break.

Lacey was a breath of fresh air for me, and there was something different about her that I couldn't quite place, but I knew it was only a matter of time before I had the chance to find out for myself.

LACEY

I had to have been a little too drunk, because sitting across from Moves filled me with the kind of urge I'd never felt before. My entire body was on fire, and the tension between us was undeniable, but before I could allow myself to get wrapped up in him, I had to at least get some information about Ortega's Autos, otherwise I would be waking up the following morning feeling like I had completely failed in what I had set out to do.

I dialed it back a bit, looking him in the eye as I told him I could use something to sober me up, and he went over to the bar to get us two glasses of water. It wasn't much, but it was enough to get the answers I needed, and I had to focus. I had to remember that I was there to collect information, and as much as I felt the urge to kiss Moves, I couldn't let myself stray too far away from what I needed.

"You know, I was out on the highway around this part of town, and my car started acting all weird, so I pulled into Ortega's. The man there was really nice in helping me out, and I was just glad to get the thing fixed. I don't have much luck with cars unfortunately," I said, and I watched his expression change completely, coming back down to earth for a moment while he tried to find a suitable answer.

"Yeah, Ortega's is a good place to go. I can put in a word for you if you ever need car assistance there again," he said, and I thought that was quite nice of him. I decided it was a good opportunity to do a bit of fishing, and I knew that it was the best time to take advantage of whatever information I could get my hands on.

"That's really nice of you, Moves. Thank you. Trust me, I'm just glad I've had this car for this long. The last one I had got stolen, and anyone I told about it said that there are places that tear those cars to pieces and sell them for parts. Though I have a hard time believing that," I said, trying to play dumb without letting him in on the fact that I suspected Ortega's of that very thing.

"I don't know of any chop shops around these parts, but if there's one thing I'm sure of, Ortega's isn't one of them. Though there's a place on the other side of town that does stuff like that. It's run by a guy by the name of El Diablo," he said, and I sat on his words for a moment, wondering where I had heard that name before.

"Well, let's just hope I manage to keep my hands on this one. It's starting to get a bit hot in here, don't you think? Would you like to join me outside for a bit of fresh air?"

That was as much information as I was going to get for now without him getting suspicious. The mention of Ortega's Autos had made his expression change, but I couldn't figure out why. He didn't seem like the type to be hiding something, and from what I've seen, Ortega's didn't seem like the place where cars got dismantled and sold for parts.

Maybe I need to broaden my search, look into that place that he told me about. Maybe there are some answers there.

We ventured outside, and I noticed there were back entrances to the bathrooms, probably for a quick stop before heading back out on the road. This place had been right off one of the major routes leading into La Playa, and I expected it got quite a bit of \traffic just about any time of the day or night.

I felt the tension return the minute Moves and I were finally alone, but I couldn't put into words what I had been feeling. My face heated up as he inched closer to me, and I watched while he scrambled to make a bit of conversation before we both jumped into something we couldn't get ourselves out of.

"It amazes me that you and your friend could come to a place like this just to have a bit of fun. I don't think I'd ever seen anyone come around these parts that weren't just passing through or spent a good chunk of their days here, but I'm glad that I was able to run into you today, Lacey," he said, inching closer to me again, and I could've sworn I was about to feel his lips press into mine, but I just had to go ahead and say something stupid.

"Yes, well, this is completely out of character for me being a lawyer and all," I said. I watched his expression change completely, going blank at the mention of my career, but I couldn't figure out why. I thought his friends would've told him what I did for a living.

"I, uh, I'm just going to head to the bathroom for a moment," I said, trying to break the awkward silence, rushing in with my heart pounding, trying to calm the urges that were welling up inside me.

Is being a lawyer really that bad? Or is there something that Moves knows that he isn't telling me? Something that would make him scared at the sound of me being involved with the law?

I leaned over the sink to catch my breath for a moment, reaching into my pocket for my phone to text Mona, because I needed to get this off my chest. I hadn't seen her for quite a while, and it dawned on me that I completely abandoned her the moment that Moves made his way over to me.

I sent the text, heading back out to see that Moves had left, and my heart sank into my stomach.

Maybe there really is more to the story after all.

MOVES

Lacey is an attorney? Did she tell anyone else about this?

I was sitting at home trying to figure out how I could've missed the signs. I'd seen her at Lily and Bailey's thinking that she was just a neighbor that they'd extended an invite to, but now I realized that she was an attorney, heavily involved with the law, and could possibly be a problem for us.

I was looking for a quick hookup, trying to blow off steam last night at the Blue Dog, but I didn't think that I'd run into Lacey. I didn't think that I would've ended up feeling that way about her either, especially seeing as we were clearly both from very different worlds. I couldn't get involved with her, not until I knew exactly what kind of attorney she was.

I hated that I had to scope her out, but I was so worried that she was going to be a problem for Chalupa's case that I had to know for sure. I had to get some information about where she worked, and I needed to know if she was anywhere close to Chalupa's case, because that would make things much more difficult.

I decided to give Hawk a call, because we needed to get a

move on finding out as much as we could. At least now we had somewhere to start.

"Hello?"

"I think I may have found us a lead that we can follow up to get some answers of our own," I said.

"What kind of lead?" Hawk sounded apprehensive.

"I met a girl at Lily and Bailey's house a while back, and I met that same girl last night at the Blue Dog, only she told me that she was an attorney. That's not going to be much of a problem if she works anywhere else, but if she's anywhere near Chalupa's case, we're going to have to find out," I explained.

"Meet me down at the underpass near the station. It's Saturday, but hopefully someone will be around that we can bump into and ask a few hard-hitting questions."

"I'll be there," I said, grabbing the keys to my bike, hopping on, and taking off into the scorching heat. I arrived at the location not long after to see Hawk pull up on his bike, nodding at me to let me know the coast was clear, and we could decide exactly how we were going to play this.

"I see you're all dressed up," I said, noticing the attire that made Hawk look entirely out of place with his jeans and a sleeved shirt that covered up all of his tattoos. It was strange to see him like that, but if we were going to try our luck, we certainly had to look the part.

"How exactly are we going to do this?" he asked.

"You're going to leave your bike here, I'm going to hang back a bit of a distance away from you while you walk down the sidewalk in front of the police station until someone comes out that you can bump into. Then make up some excuse, something involving Lacey. Anything that can confirm that she works there," I instructed, and he nodded.

We made our way back up, and I hid our bikes in an alleyway while I got close enough to hear what he was saying as he hung around the corner waiting for someone to come out. It didn't take as long as I thought it would, and I spotted a police officer coming out of the building just as Hawk moved in to bump directly into him.

"Oh my God, I'm so sorry," he said, as the police officer kindly let him know that it was all right.

"Are you heading in there?" he asked politely.

"Yes, actually I just wanted to see if Lacey was in today. She's helping me out with a bit of advice seeing as my wife and I are having a few problems. I live in the apartment across from hers, I know it's terrible of me to show up unannounced like this, at her place of work, but she told me to stop by if I ever needed and she'd see me when she was on her break," I heard Hawk say, and it was a ridiculous excuse, but it seemed to be enough to get the response we needed out of the officer.

"I'm sorry, she's not in her office today," he said, and from the look on his face, I could tell that he was trying to process what Hawk had said, but he'd already left the scene, walking off and not looking back.

It was a strange scenario, especially because it wasn't the kind of place that anyone could just show up to, and I knew it was only a matter of time before that news traveled back to Lacey, but I'd gotten the answer I was looking for.

Maybe he won't think anything of it. Maybe he's going to forget about the whole thing the moment he gets back to work.

Meeting back up with Hawk, I had to tease him about his choice of excuse.

"You do realize that people don't just pop in to see their friends at the LPPD, right?" I asked, laughing while we both got back onto our bikes.

"What else was I supposed to say, man? I had to look desperate enough. He didn't seem to care much, so I don't think that he's going to be telling anyone. He doesn't look like the kind of person that knows her too well." I hoped he was right.

I couldn't help the feelings that were welling up inside of me, and I tried my best to put the thought from my mind that Lacey had been an attorney all the time, and that she was involved with Chalupa's case. It was truly too bad because I found myself really wanting her, and I could almost feel the warmth of her skin on mine, but sadly, I was never going to be able to experience that for myself.

Even if I could imagine her being a wildcat in bed, I couldn't allow myself to get involved with someone who had completely different priorities than I did, and now that I was sure where her priorities were, I thought it best to stay far away from her.

I was sure that the little stunt that Hawk and I had pulled was going to ruffle some feathers, that is if the police officer that Hawk spoke to even bothered to mention that someone was there looking for Lacey on her day off. I didn't count on the fact that he was going to keep his mouth shut, but I knew it was genuinely a possibility.

On Monday I got onto my bike, hearing the sound of the engine roar through the sky while I headed deep into the heart of La Playa to meet with the attorney that my brother had directed me to. I could only hope that he was going to be some help to us, because I couldn't imagine how much longer Chalupa could take lying low until it was time to face trial, especially because he had nothing to do with the stolen car in the first place.

Every time I allow myself to think about the fact that someone was out there trying to get under our skin, I felt my blood boil. I was furious, frustrated, and I couldn't wait to put all of this behind us.

I was prepared to do just about anything to make sure that Chalupa got out and the Outlaw Souls were safe from prying eyes.

We didn't engage in terrible, malicious behavior like Las Balas did, and I made sure that we never dabbled in the kind of horrific things they spent their days doing. We tried to keep a low profile, look out for our own, and not stick our noses where they didn't belong.

It seemed that whoever was behind this didn't care much about the fact that we never caused much trouble for anyone around us, because it didn't stop them from wanting to frame the Outlaw Souls for something we didn't even do.

I'm running out of time, and Chalupa is going to need proper representation if he's going to stay out of jail.

I pulled up at the location that my brother gave me and hopped off my bike, knocked on the door of what appeared to be a small set of offices, and waited patiently for the man to open up the door.

When he finally did and I got a good look at him, I couldn't believe my eyes. He didn't seem like the kind of shark we were looking for, one that would stop at nothing to make sure that Chalupa was able to walk out of the courtroom a free man, and I was even more terrified to see just how much torment we were going to have to suffer through before this was all over.

"You must be Michael," he said. "Your brother said you would be stopping by, though up until recently I didn't even know that Keith had a brother. Let's just say you're not the guy I expected." He stared down at my tattoos, probably wondering whether Keith and I were actually blood relatives or not.

"Yes, he told me that you could help me with a case. My

friend has been wrongfully accused of stealing a car, and now he's going to be put on trial. He's desperately in need of representation and I'm hoping that you will be willing to represent him," I said, searching his expression for any sign of apprehension.

"Why don't you come in and we'll talk about the details," he said, and I followed him into the little office, immediately hit with the scent of week-old air freshener, lukewarm coffee, and printer ink. It certainly didn't feel like the kind of promising opportunity that we were looking for, but with the money we had, we just couldn't be too picky.

Keith probably recommended him because he believed it would be our best bet versus using a public defense attorney who wouldn't care about Chalupa in the slightest.

I have to keep an open mind and believe that this guy is going to get us one step closer to bringing Chalupa home, otherwise I'm going to go insane with the amount of worry that's coursing through me right now.

LACEY

My head is killing me.

The minute my eyelids fluttered open, I blinked away the blurriness of my vision until I was able to sit upright in bed again. My entire body ached like I'd just been hit by a truck, and I was starting to wonder just how much fun I'd truly allowed myself to have when I was supposed to be gathering information on Ortega's Autos.

I couldn't think straight, dragging myself to the bathroom to splash some water on my face before heading into the kitchen for some pain medicine.

My stomach turned at the thought of eating anything, but I didn't want to go through the rest of my day feeling weak, so I opened up the fridge to find something edible. I made myself a cup of tea, filling a glass of water alongside it so I could stay hydrated and get back to feeling like myself again.

I looked over at the couch to where Mona was still sleeping, and I decided to fix breakfast for her as well, to thank her for going out with me last night, even if I didn't get as much information as I would've liked.

I cracked two eggs into a pan, stirring them around

briskly before popping some bread into the toaster. I heard Mona start to stir on the couch, kicking off the blanket that was around her feet before sitting up and rubbing her eyes.

"Someone slept in rather late," I teased, and she looked just as confused as I was.

"We did have a wild night after all. I needed my beauty rest," she said, and I couldn't agree more. If there was one thing I remembered, it was putting away drink after drink, trying to get out of my head for a little while, and prove to everyone in the room that I was capable of enjoying myself. I needed to blend in if I was going to get information.

I only hoped that Mona would've been able to tell me more about what happened last night, because my memories were all fuzzy and I couldn't tell what was real from what wasn't anymore.

"Come here, eat something. We both have quite a lot of recovering to do," I said, and she nodded, joining me at the small breakfast nook, where we attacked our plates, trying to get down as much food as possible without feeling the urge to puke it all out.

"So how wild exactly was last night? I don't even remember how we got home," I said, biting into my toast.

"I hooked up with one of the guys in the parking lot, and his friend gave us a lift home in his truck. He was quite nice, though I can't seem to remember his name," Mona said, and I laughed. It was then that I remembered that I'd almost had a similar experience, though the man I'd met wasn't a stranger. He was someone that I'd met before, and as I pictured his face, the memories all began to flood back in.

I remembered that we had almost kissed, and that I rushed into the bathroom, only to come out to find that he was gone. There was something strange about our last interaction, and I couldn't stop dwelling on the fact that he looked like he'd seen a ghost the moment I told him that I was a lawyer.

"We're going to have to go back to get my car," Mona said, gulping down her glass of water before she reached over for the pain medication herself.

"We will, don't worry," I told her, lost in thought about the interaction I'd had with Moves. I knew that the only people who would run after hearing that I was a lawyer would be someone who had something to hide.

I still had no idea what was going on down at Ortega's Autos, but Moves seemed to know quite a bit about another place on the other side of town where cars went to be dismantled and destroyed. I had to believe that Moves knew more than he was letting on, and I was determined to find out exactly what that was, but I didn't have any way of contacting him.

I don't even know if he's going to see me now that he knows I'm a lawyer. He might be deliberately trying to stay out of sight so I don't catch on to the fact that he and his buddies are hiding something.

Mona looked up at me like she was starting to remember more about her night too.

"What's that look?" I asked her.

"I believe that guy I hooked up with had told me that he was a patch for a club called the Outlaw Souls," she said.

"The Outlaw Souls?"

"They're a biker gang, and their favorite stomping ground seems to be the Blue Dog. That's why we felt so out of place when we were there. We were probably the only people there that didn't own a shiny hunk of metal," she said.

"Did your biker friend tell you anything else about the club he belongs to?"

"He told me that a bunch of them work down at Ortega's Autos," she said, and I could see her starting to put the pieces together in her head.

I wondered if Moves had also been working at Ortega's Autos, and that would give me reason to believe that he certainly did know more than he was letting on. I was determined to find out what that was, but the only person that was going to be able to get close to them now would be Mona, because I had a feeling that Moves wasn't going to want to see me.

"I think there may be a way that we can get to the bottom of this, Mona. If you'd be willing to meet up with your biker friend again, entice him a little more, maybe get a few more answers about what really goes on at Ortega's Autos, it can really help me start to put the pieces together." I thought for a moment that she was going to think it was a terrible idea and shoot me down right on the spot, but she stared back at me with a smile, and I knew she was going to be up for the job.

"If I can sleep with that guy, I'm definitely in. He was incredibly hot, and I don't think anyone has ever taken me for more of a ride than he could. He is a biker after all," she said, and I laughed.

"You're crazy, you know that? Well, you already know that I think sex is overrated, but whatever floats your boat. If you'd be willing to get some more information for me, I would be eternally grateful," I said with a smile.

"One of these days someone is going to come along and change your mind, Lacey. You just wait. Though I would love to do a little snooping for you. We'll find out what's really going on there soon enough."

MOVES

I'm starting to get a little antsy because I'm afraid that we're not going to get anywhere in time for Chalupa's case to go to trial. If we don't come up with some substantial evidence, or find out who is really behind this, then we can kiss our freedom goodbye. If they take one of us down, it's only a matter of time before they get to the rest of us, and we can't let that happen.

I arrived at Hawk's place that morning so we could start discussing the case, because we were running out of time, and we needed to get ahead of this before things eventually got worse.

When Hawk opened the door, he looked rather distraught, like he hadn't slept in days, and I wondered what had gotten him looking so rough. It was just a few days ago that we were riding together, trying to figure out whether the girl I'd met at the bar was working for the government.

He opened the door wide so I could step inside, and I noticed that his house was much emptier than usual. I usually saw his wife roaming around, asking us if we needed anything before we headed out for the day, and I truly appreciated her hospitality, but the look in Hawk's eyes told me that something terrible had happened, and he just didn't seem to be in the mood to talk about the case at all.

"What's the matter, Hawk?" I asked him, and he led me to sit down in his living room, where I waited patiently for him to tell me what was going on.

"There's something I didn't tell you when we went out on our little mission a few days ago, but I hooked up with a young chick there the other night when we were out at the bar, and it was the first time in a long time that I felt alive." He looked at me with a pained expression. I nodded for him to continue. "It wasn't until then that I realized just how terrible my marriage has been lately, and that it was hanging on by a thread, but it was evident that I wasn't going to be able to keep it a secret forever." Hawk was obviously finding this difficult. Although we were close, no, we were family, we didn't talk to each other much about our private lives. We never opened up about emotional issues.

"She left me, Moves, and she had every right to. I thought that I was going to be much more broken up watching her walk right out that door, but I wasn't. I felt relieved, and I know how selfish that sounds, but I just can't help myself."

I sat there completely understanding how he felt. I'd never been with one woman long enough to know what love actually felt like, but if there was one thing I could tell was that Hawk and his wife had changed over the years. They weren't the same people they had been when they got married, and I'd had a feeling something like this was going to happen eventually.

"Maybe it was for the best, Hawk. If that girl made you feel alive again, made you feel like your life was worth living, then maybe it was a good thing that you two had that moment together, because you wouldn't want to live out the rest of your days feeling trapped in your marriage, and neither would your wife," I said, and he nodded at me.

"I know what I did was wrong, but to be truthful, I don't regret a moment. The only thing is, I don't even know if I'm gonna see that chick again. It was a one-night stand, and we both knew that. Wham bam thank you ma'am," he chuckled.

"Listen, Hawk. I think you should ask her out. Did you at least catch her name?" I asked.

"Her name is Mona, like the painting."

"Oh, great."

"What is it?"

"That's Lacey's best friend. Like, the Lacey we just found out is an attorney at the DA's office. Though it's quite possible that Mona has absolutely nothing to do with how Lacey chooses to do her job, and in that case, I don't see a problem with you seeing her again," I said. "You just need to be careful, that's all."

"I'll keep an eye out for anything suspicious, but I don't even think she'd be interested in a guy like me. What could I offer her? She's definitely out of my league," he said, but even I didn't believe that.

"You have to give yourself a little more credit, Hawk. You're never going to know until you try. So if the opportunity presents itself again, I say go for it."

Hawk nodded. "Okay, so now back to business. How did the meeting go with the contact that you had?"

"It was terrible. He didn't seem like the kind of guy that would do anything to get Chalupa out, but I believe that my brother only recommended him because he was better than a public defense attorney, and no one else in their right mind was going to take the case out of the goodness of their heart," I explained.

"Man, I really hope that this is going to work because I can't imagine what's going to happen if Chalupa gets put away." Hawk sighed. "It's going to give whoever is behind this the green light to keep framing us until every single last one of us is behind bars. We can't allow that to happen, and if we want to have any chance of clearing Chalupa's name, we're going to have to solve this on our own."

"We're gonna get to the bottom of this. There is no way we're letting Chalupa live out the rest of his days in jail for something he didn't do. We'll find out who's really behind this, and we're going to make them pay," I said, and Hawk smiled.

We have our work cut out for us, but hopefully we're going to start getting a few answers very soon. We have to, otherwise we're all going to be taken down.

LACEY

I was getting ready to head to work that morning when I heard a knock on my bedroom door. I opened it up to see Mona standing there. After our last chat, she'd decided to stay over for a few days to help me out with the case. I knew she was more than a little apprehensive about getting into bed with a biker, both literally and figuratively, but I needed to know she was still up for it. I still needed some more information on what they were really doing while working at Ortega's Autos.

I led her over to my bed where she could sit and tell me all of the things that were on her mind while I slipped into my two-piece gray suit, pulling my hair back into a low bun and collecting my case files to stuff into my bag.

"You seem a bit on edge, Mona. Are you having second thoughts about seeing that guy again?" I asked, worried that she was going to want to back out.

"No, I'm sure I'll be able to find something out for you, but I just want you to know that I might be treading on dangerous ground here," she confessed. "I've never dated a guy that was this much older than me, but there's something really sweet about him. He seems really gentle and kind, but I'm scared that I'm going to regret it if I get in a little too deep." I could see the excitement behind her eyes, and I knew she was going to regret it if she didn't at least take a chance on the guy.

"I have to thank you for even agreeing to go snooping around when you're supposed to be enjoying your time out with this nice guy, but I have to say, as your friend, I think you should go for it. This is the happiest I've seen you in such a long time, and I don't want you to lose that," I said, and she smiled.

"I'm glad I have your support right now because I really feel like I'm in it a little over my head," she said. "I don't know the first thing about his world, about what's considered okay and what isn't, but I'm sure I'm going to be finding out soon enough, especially if I'm going to be scoping out the people he keeps closest to him."

"I've had this feeling in the pit of my stomach ever since we left there that there's more to all of this than we may realize," I said. "I just want you to be careful, because I can't imagine that they're going to take too kindly to finding out that you're snooping."

She smiled back at me, heeding that warning. "I promise that I'm going to stay in touch, and I'll keep you posted if I find anything that will be of use to you," she assured me.

"Thanks, Mona. I don't know what I'd do without you because I know I blew my opportunity to find out what was going on through Moves." I was quite sad because there was a part of me that felt like there was a connection between us, and now all of that was lost because he'd found out what I did for a living. I was starting to feel like my curiosity was getting the better of me, because I wanted nothing more than to know why he'd taken off after learning about my occupation.

I worried that he was involved in something that I wasn't able to pick up on, something dangerous that would prove to be a problem for the rest of his friends, and thus mine as well. I could only hope that Mona was capable of watching her back, because I'd never be able to forgive myself if something happened to her.

I had to be strong, keep my head held high, and get back to work because the DA was going to want an update on how the case was progressing. The information I had was barely anything, but I had a few leads now that I could follow up on, and it was up to me to see them through until I happened upon something substantial.

I arrived at the office not long after, making myself a quick cup of coffee because I'd skipped breakfast. I felt the warm liquid trickle down my throat, jolting me back to life. I heard a knock on my office door and the receptionist popped her head in, telling me that the DA would like to see me in his office.

I knew he was going to want an update on the case. I was scared to tell him that I didn't have much to offer, but I knew he was going to tell me to keep looking until I found something. When I knocked on his door and entered, he motioned for me to sit so he could grill me on whatever it is I was able to find.

"How's the case going, Lacey?" he asked, and I bit my lip nervously before I told him the truth.

"I haven't found any evidence that Ortega's Autos is a chop shop, so maybe the guy that was arrested for stealing that car was operating on his own agenda. I searched nearly every inch of that place and there was no way that they were destroying cars anywhere near there. Though I did find out that there is a place on the other end of town where a chop shop might be located. It's owned by someone named El Diablo, but I have yet to find out more."

He didn't look too impressed by my lack of evidence, even though he'd given me quite the strict time frame.

"Lacey, I know that you're new to undercover work, but I expect better from you, especially seeing your skills in other areas of your job. I know that you're treading lightly because you're afraid to piss off the wrong people, but I'm going to be frank with you. That's exactly what you need to do to start getting the answers you want. What you have so far just isn't good enough, and if you want to keep your job, you're going to have to find better evidence soon. Is that clear?"

I nodded. "Crystal."

"Good, now get back to work."

I left his office feeling like a complete and utter failure for the fact that I'd let myself get too wrapped up in the allure of the situation that I wasn't able to find anything that would point me in the right direction. I was starting to feel like maybe I wasn't cut out for this kind of position, especially seeing as how difficult it was to get anyone to talk around that part of town.

I knew that the DA wasn't going to let me out of it so easily, and I didn't want my incompetence to affect how I proceed in my job, so I had to find something that would be deemed worthwhile.

I headed back into my office, sitting at my desk with my head in my hands trying to figure out what my next move was going to be. I couldn't just show up to Ortega's with more car trouble expecting that they weren't going to catch on to the fact that I was trying to snoop, especially because there was one of them that already knew what I did for a living, and he'd surely be able to expose me before I learned anything that would help. I knew that I had to get back to Ortega's and find an angle that was going to be able to work. I just had to figure out how.

I was so lost in thought that I didn't even hear the knock at my office door, and Richard peeked his head in.

"Someone's not having a good day, huh?" he said. "Why the glum face?"

"Richard, I really can't do this right now." I sighed. "I'm struggling. I have no idea how I'm going to get any of those people down at the auto shop to trust me. Some of them must already be on to me, and I'm being pushed to find evidence that I'm not even sure exists in the first place."

He hung on every word, even though I knew he was still quite envious that the DA had given me this case instead of him. He wasn't the type of person to allow that to come between us professionally.

"If you want them to believe that you're not there to expose them, you're going to have to give them a reason to trust you, Lacey. I know that's hard to hear because up until this point you've never done any undercover work before, but you're going to have to believe it if you want them to. That's just how it has to be."

I knew there was truth in his words, it was just incredibly depressing, knowing how terrible and unfit for the job I felt.

"Do you really think I'm going to be able to pull this off?" I asked, glancing up at him.

"I still think that I would've done a better job, but yes. I think you're capable enough to get what you need and get out before anyone finds out what you're really doing there."

"Thank you, Richard. I hope it's not too late for that."

"Any time, Lacey," he replied, leaving me alone while I gathered my things, taking a deep breath and heading back out to my car so I could make the drive down to Ortega's. I didn't have a plan, I didn't know what I was going to do, but I could only hope that I figured something out before I pulled up there unannounced.

MOVES

Hawk and I rode alongside each other, enjoying the early morning wind while we were on our way to Ortega's to talk to Ryder. I was worried that he wasn't going to be able to help us much, because we still weren't able to collect many clues that would point us in the direction of the people who were framing us.

I told myself to stay calm, trying to convince myself that we were going to make it out of this before anyone else got hurt. I had to believe that, otherwise I was going to dwell on the possibility that it would be the end of the Outlaw Souls as we knew it, and I certainly wasn't going to stand for that.

It was a difficult situation because we had no idea who or what we were up against. If we at least knew who had tipped off the LPPD on Chalupa's whereabouts, and how they were able to plant evidence on him that would convince the police that he had something to do with the stolen car, we could've at least retaliated with force. I was starting to think that we were going to need a different approach if we wanted to make sure that no harm came to Chalupa while we dealt with this.

When we arrived at Ortega's, I could already tell that the

tension was high, and every face I caught sight of looked just as worried as I felt. They couldn't put into words what they were feeling, but the uncertainty was starting to get to them in a way they wouldn't be able to understand. Many of them still had a lot to learn about how we dealt with threats, about how we managed to stay out of trouble even though there were always going to be people trying to take us down. I was just worried that one of them was going to crack and sell us out if they were ever caught under pressure. Even though I managed to enforce the rules, I couldn't possibly keep track of everybody, especially when my main focus was trying to get Chalupa his freedom.

We walked into the garage, hit with the scent of sweat, oil, and rubber the minute we got inside. I looked around for Ryder, but the first pair of eyes I caught weren't his. They were Chalupa's.

"What are you doing back here? I thought I told you to lay low until we came to fetch you." I could see the fear in his eyes, and I knew there was probably a part of him that believed he wasn't going to get out of this without jail time.

"I'm scared, Moves. I don't know what's going to happen to me, or to any of us because of what the LPPD thinks I'm doing. I'm just glad that at least you all believe that I didn't do it, but I still can't figure out how they would've had enough evidence to make the arrest."

I glanced over to see Ryder approach with a dirty washcloth in his hands, wiping the oil off of his fingers.

"We know you didn't do it, Chalupa," Ryder said, throwing the rag on the bench, "but that doesn't mean that this is just going to go away on its own. I'm tired of not knowing who's framing us, and if it were up to me I would've stormed the Las Balas compound by now demanding answers."

I knew that he was just operating on fear, and that

confronting our rivals at this time wasn't going to achieve anything.

"That's why you're not in charge of this, Ryder," I said. "You don't know for sure that they were behind this, and if we find out that they had nothing to do with this, but we went ahead and ambushed them anyway, we're going to have more problems on our hands than we're going to be able to handle."

Ryder nodded in reluctant agreement. "Come on, let's go inside the office to get out of the heat and talk about this further."

He led us into the back, where we could enjoy a little air conditioning while we discussed how we were going to go about finding the evidence we needed to set Chalupa free. Ryder opened the cooler and took out four beers, opened them up, and handed them to us while we indulged, each of us lost in our thoughts about what to do.

"I don't see how we're going to find any evidence if we don't head back to the scene," Hawk said, and even though I knew he was right, I still thought that it was way too risky.

"They probably still have cops canvassing that area, waiting for one of us to show up there asking the wrong questions or displaying any sort of suspicious behavior," I explained, and we all sat there for a moment in complete silence while we thought about what to do.

"Well, you guys are just going to have to do a better job of sneaking around, because until we find something substantial we're just going to be sitting on our asses all day waiting for the inevitable," Ryder said, and I nodded.

"We're going to figure something out, and we're going to keep you out of jail, Chalupa," I said. "I know that you're worried, but the LPPD are not locking you up for something you had no involvement in, okay?" Chalupa nodded, gulping at the thought.

"I already told you I won't be able to last a day in prison," he said.

"Oh, we know," Ryder said.

Hearing a knock on his office door, he opened it up to see Lily and Bailey there dropping off lunch that Paige had sent. I was so grateful to them because I was absolutely starving, and I couldn't remember the last time I'd had anything to eat.

We sat there for a little while enjoying our meal, but we were interrupted moments later to hear the bell ring, indicating that there was a customer that needed service. Ryder had been working hard all morning, so I decided to help him out a little and take this one off his hands. He thanked me, and I ventured out to the front to see who needed assistance, and just how long the job was actually going to take me.

I stopped in my tracks when I caught sight of the face staring back at me.

"You?"

LACEY

This is a stupid idea. I didn't even pull out any parts from my car this time. They are not going to believe I have car trouble for one second, so I better come up with something fast.

Hearing the bell ring overhead, I waited patiently for someone to come out to help me. It felt like ages before the door opened, but when I glanced up at the man standing before me, I was truly shocked. I hadn't even thought about the possibility that Moves could be there, and it made me feel even more uneasy now that he could see right through me. He was a smart man, and I could already tell that he was suspicious about the fact that I just turned up unannounced.

I was worried that he was going to call everyone out here, expose me for being a lawyer, and then proceed to tell them that I was working for the DA. I already had a hunch that he knew, but I wasn't going to be sure until he told me himself.

"What are you doing here?" he asked, and I didn't know how to answer him, but I knew I had to think of something quick.

"I came to apologize, Moves. I know that we left things abruptly the other night after I told you what I do for a living, but I didn't think that would be much of a problem for you," I said to him, watching his cold exterior start to soften the more I spoke.

"It is a problem for me, Lacey. As nice of a girl as you are, I just can't see myself getting involved with you now, especially knowing that you're a lawyer," he said, making it sound like it was the worst thing in the world.

"Why is that?" I asked, trying not to pry too much to the point where he started to believe that I had an ulterior motive.

"It's more complicated than I can explain right now, and I think it's best that we don't talk about it anymore."

As he spoke, everyone else came out to join us. I caught sight of Lily and Bailey, realizing that they all belonged to the Outlaw Souls. I hadn't put the pieces together at first, but now I began to see that they were all like a family around here. The biker the LPPD had picked up was there too, although he was hanging back, trying to look inconspicuous. At the party, I guessed they didn't connect me with the case. Why would they? I was just a lawyer. But after what had happened since then, I was sure Moves would fill in the blanks for them.

"Oh my God, Lacey!" screamed Lily, heading in to embrace me, until she stood back and had a look at the expression of everyone else in the room, realizing that there was something going on there that she didn't initially pick up on.

"It's nice to see you all again. I recognize each of your faces, except for yours," I said, turning to the mysterious older man, but I had a hunch I knew exactly who he was.

"You guys can go ahead, we got this," Moves said, and they all took off except for him and the mystery man.

"I'm not sure I know your name, but I think you might be the man that had a really nice time with my best friend. She just can't seem to stop talking about you. She's been wanting to get in touch with you again, and I can tell that she likes you, so why don't I give you her number?" I offered, and the man nodded.

"My name is Hawk, and thank you. That would be very kind," he said, and I smiled, scribbling Mona's number down on a piece of paper and handing it to him. He immediately took off in the other direction, and I could see him pulling out his cell phone in the corner of my eye.

"I think the two of them really did hit it off," I said, trying to lighten the mood between Moves and me, even though I was quite sure he was still undecided about me.

"You really are something, Lacey. I don't know what it is about you, but you don't seem like the type of lawyer that wants to cause trouble. You see, we've dealt with a lot of dirty cops and lawyers trying to put us behind bars for things we had no involvement in for a very long time, so forgive me for being quite harsh earlier. I'm just looking out for everyone else around here," he said, and it was nice to know that he was so protective of them all.

"Trust me, I'm not here to cause any trouble. I may be a lawyer by occupation, but right now I'm just a friend trying to help my best friend get in touch with the guy she likes," I said, lying through my teeth.

"Well, I appreciate you coming down here to do that," he said. I thought that we were starting to get somewhere, but all he did was lead me back to my car and bid me goodbye. I took off, knowing that if I stayed trying to sniff around, Moves was going to start to suspect me. Right now, I needed him to trust me if I was going to get more evidence and find out what was really happening around there.

I could tell that he was still a bit uneasy, and when I left Ortega's, I felt my stomach turn at the thought of how Moves made me feel. He made it incredibly clear that he couldn't get involved with someone like me, but I couldn't ignore the fact that I was starting to feel quite attracted to him, even if I wasn't sure what his involvement was in all of this.

I wanted to believe that everyone there had been innocent and that I was just trying to fill in the blanks, but I knew I had to stay alert. I didn't want to find myself thinking about a man that could possibly have been involved in breaking the law, and until I was sure that he or the other members of the Outlaw Souls had anything to do with the stolen car and chop shop allegations, I couldn't allow myself to consider any kind of relationship with him.

I returned home that night to find Mona in the kitchen making dinner. It was the first time I'd seen her lift a finger around the house willingly in a while, and I could already tell by the smile on her face that Hawk had reached out to her. I was glad that in the middle of all of this, she'd found some happiness, and I just wanted her to be careful because I wouldn't be able to live with myself if she got involved in something dangerous. I knew that she was doing everything she could to help me out with the case, even though she didn't have to, and I appreciated her so much for sticking out her neck for me.

"I take it that me giving Hawk your number wasn't a mistake?" I asked teasingly.

"Thank you, Lacey. I truly didn't know when I was going to see him again, and while we haven't quite worked out those details yet, it's certainly a start," she said.

"I'm just glad you're happy, Mona. Though I don't think I've ever seen you so happy that you opted to cook instead of ordering in," I said.

She grinned at me. "I know it's a bit of a shock, but I wanted to treat my best friend for supporting me through this, because you're not the only one that hasn't been dating much lately. I'm not sure that anything substantial is going to come from it, but I'm willing to try."

I was glad that she still had a healthy amount of doubt, especially because she wouldn't be able to be sure that he wasn't involved in any criminal activity until she found out for herself. I hated that I had to count on her to find out these things instead of it being the other way around, but I just had to make sure that I did everything I could to protect her.

She was indulging in a little young infatuation, giddy, excited, and ready for just about anything. I didn't want to take any of that away from her on account of a few suspicions that really didn't have much merit at that point. I promised myself that I was going to hold out at least until I knew more, or until she found out something that would prove that Ortega's was in fact harboring criminal activity.

"Please, sit. I need your advice on how exactly this date might go," she said, and I took the seat next to her, talking about all the things she loved about this guy. I tried to keep my head up, to not let her in on the fact that I was worried she was making a terrible mistake even though I needed her to stay in touch with Hawk so I could keep an eye on the rest of the Outlaw Souls.

I was also under a lot of pressure from the DA to see this case through, and if I turned up empty-handed at the end of this, he was going to take what was left of my career to the chopping block.

I was aware that I never spoke highly of my job because it truly wasn't my first choice, but I knew that it felt good to bring down the bad guys that deserved to be behind bars. Now I was starting to feel differently about my place in all of this, I wondered how I would've reacted if it was Moves that had been arrested versus a random biker that I didn't know. I wanted to think that I would remain neutral, that I wouldn't pick sides even though it was my job to side with justice, but

I couldn't help but feel like I was leaning toward the latter. I worried that this case was going to change me as both a lawyer and a human being. I could already feel the increasing tension between Moves and me, and I wasn't quite sure whether that was due to both of us trying not to ruffle the other one's feathers, or if it was because deep down Moves had begun to feel something for me too.

I couldn't deny that I was attracted to him, that I was starting to fall for the allure of his world and everything that came with it, but I knew I couldn't get too close, otherwise I was going to lose everything I'd worked so hard to protect.

MOVES

What the hell is Lacey doing sniffing around Ortega's? If she's looking for answers about Chalupa, she's not going to find them by trying to scope us out. I still wonder why she's alone on this job, and why no one else from her department has shown up to take some of the edge off. I'm starting to wonder whether she really doesn't have much involvement in Chalupa's case, and that she's only here because she's curious. Either way, I have to be smart about my interactions with her, otherwise I'm probably going to end up regretting it.

I was making my way down to Hawk's place so we could go try to find some proof that Chalupa was innocent.

We just needed to point them in a different direction, show them that they had the wrong guy, and instead of trying to crack down on us, they should be looking for the people who actually deserved to be behind bars. I ran my fingers through my hair, feeling the sweat on my forehead as the sun over La Playa was beating down on me overhead.

I felt uneasy, especially after my run-in with Lacey. I was still trying to figure out what her intentions were, and if she was trying to find out the truth alone. It was a stupid decision to have her around us all if she was trying to find evidence to prove that we were somehow involved in grand theft auto.

I couldn't be sure, but I also knew that even after knowing that she was working at the DA's office, and even after knowing that there was a possibility she was trying to take us all down, I couldn't help but feel attracted to her.

Every time I was around her, all I could focus on were those beautiful eyes of hers staring up at me, the fullness of her lips, or the extraordinary curves of her body. I thought about how close I was to kissing her that night at the bar before I found out the truth about her, and I was starting to wish that I did. She was so captivating whenever she was around, and nobody in the room could keep their eyes off her, and I hated that I found myself being strangely protective of her even though I knew it wasn't my place to act that way.

I had to separate my budding feelings from how I had to see her in order to keep working toward the truth, otherwise I was probably going to end up doing something I would regret.

I could feel the tension between us whenever we were together, and that alone told me that there was a part of her that felt the same. I wished I could explore that, but I knew I had to start focusing on getting back to thinking about Chalupa's freedom, otherwise that distraction would be the very reason he'd end up behind bars. I'd promised him that I wasn't going to let that happen, and I had to make sure that no harm came his way. I felt it in my gut that Las Balas had something to do with this, and even though I had to stay neutral to the rest of the Outlaw Souls to prevent any unwanted confrontation, it didn't stop me from wanting to storm into their hideout and find out the truth for myself.

I sighed, realizing that I was going to have to wait because Hawk and I were going to head back to the street where

Chalupa had been arrested, hoping to find something that would bring us closer to this all finally being over.

"Hey, Moves. You ready to head out?" Hawk asked, opening up his front door. I could tell that he appeared a lot more chipper, like things were going well between him and Lacey's best friend, but I still had to do my part and warn him to be careful around her. It was quite possible that Mona would be reporting back to Lacey about their little dates, and I had to make sure that there was no incriminating information being shared among them.

"Well, don't you look happy. I take it you had the chance to talk to Mona?"

"We're playing it by ear, but right now we need to find something that's going to keep Chalupa out of prison." I wondered if he was trying to avoid the subject on purpose.

"You're right. Let's go." We both hopped onto our bikes, revving our engines before we took off, heading into the heart of La Playa to find the exact spot where Chalupa had been arrested. I could tell that Hawk and I both were a little afraid to be there, because if we were spotted by police, there was the possibility we wouldn't be able to get away in time.

I had to remind myself to stay alert, to not let any of the distractions swimming around my mind find their way back in, otherwise it could've potentially caused more problems that we certainly weren't equipped to handle.

I glanced over at Hawk as we pulled our bikes into an alleyway not far from the area where Chalupa was arrested. We looked out, checking that the coast was clear. It was strange that anyone would've even been able to tip the police off knowing that cars didn't usually get stolen around these parts. It was mostly a commercial area, and there were eyes everywhere, so I wondered how many people they had been able to convince to be an eye-witness to Chalupa stealing the car, because that was the only logical explanation.

We looked around, recognizing all of the familiar places we used to spend time in before we moved out closer to the Blue Dog. It was a nice reminder that things were quiet and calm in the past, but the longer we ran, the more trouble we seemed to find ourselves in even if we didn't go looking for it. It dawned on me that we would never truly escape that kind of trouble, because there were always going to be people coming after us, hoping to take us down in order to take our places.

It felt like ages, while Hawk and I searched every corner, going through trash, canvassing the entire area to make sure that we didn't miss anything. Everything seemed to be rather normal until I made my way to the front of the convenience store, reaching down and picking up something that someone had to have unknowingly left behind.

"Hawk, I think you need to come see this. I believe I found something."

LACEY

I could feel the warmth of his fingertips brush against my bare skin, reaching over the curve of my breasts, while he worked his way down my body. Something about it felt dangerous, spontaneous, and unlike anything I'd ever done before, but I lay there under him, biting my lip in anticipation of what he was going to do next. He stared down at me, his eyes lowering to my lips, pressing into mine while his tongue reached into my mouth playfully. I was bursting with the idea of what we were about to do, but before the fun could finally begin, I woke up.

I jumped up in bed, clutching my covers as I realized that I'd just had a wet dream about Moves, and that was only going to make things that much more complicated. I couldn't understand why this was all starting to hit me now, and I could only hope that I wouldn't have to run into him for a long time, at least until I could get this out of my system.

I sat there in bed with the strong feeling washing over me that Ortega's was clean, and that it was never a chop shop to begin with. I couldn't put that gut feeling into words, but I knew it wasn't going to be enough to convince any of the people who were working on this case with me. They were all back at the station waiting for the DA to give the go-ahead to start making arrests, and I knew they all just wanted an excuse to put those bikers behind bars even if they didn't have any part in what was going on. I was starting to question whether I should even trust my gut, or if I only felt that way because I had the hots for an Outlaw Soul. I wanted to tap into my lawyer instincts, but it was much easier said than done these days.

My focus had shifted entirely from trying to find the truth about Ortega's, which at the time sounded like a much easier task, than now wondering whether Moves and the rest of the Outlaw Souls had any involvement in criminal activity at all.

I wondered what I would do if I did in fact find out that they were engaging in illegal work, because I wouldn't be able to crack down on them myself, but I wasn't sure I even wanted to. My newfound feelings for Moves were starting to cloud my judgment in ways I hadn't expected them to, and I didn't want to spend the entire time distracted by what the thought of his touch was going to be like.

I had to find a way to re-center myself, to think about why the DA had given me the case in the first place, but it was Richard that had told me I needed to get creative with my approaches, and that had only landed me in more trouble.

I thought about going to the DA with that hunch of mine, but I knew he would have me escorted out of his office on the grounds that I was just wasting his time. He truly believed that there was more going on at Ortega's than met the eye, and while that might be true, it didn't mean it was necessarily criminal.

I wonder what must be going through Moves' head right about now, because if he has any suspicions about me, I can only imagine that he'd want to get close to find out more.

Ever since I let it slip that I was a lawyer, he'd been very hard to read, withdrawn, and shut off from everyone around him. It was going to make things a lot more difficult if I ran into him again before this was over, but I had to keep trying, because the future of my job depended on it.

I hated that I couldn't go at this the same way that Mona could, because no one had any suspicions about her, and she could get as close as she needed to in order to find out the right information, but she might not necessarily know what to look out for. I could've coached her all I wanted, but it wasn't going to change the fact that there might be very important things that she was going to miss on account of actually being wrapped up in her very own distraction.

I was just going to have to find another way to get close to Moves and charm him enough that I could find out whether or not Ortega's was actually clean. I wanted to believe that, because it would help me justify the feelings that were growing every day for Moves, and there was a part of me that wanted nothing more than to just explore them.

I stayed home from the office that day to go over the evidence from the arrests that were made one more time, trying to decide whether or not there was something I might have missed now that I had a bit more knowledge of the Outlaw Souls and their involvement with all of this. I was thumbing through countless papers, rereading each of the suspects' statements, but they all denied any involvement whatsoever. I knew that could very well be because they didn't want to own up to what they did, but I was starting to feel differently about it all.

I looked down at the picture of the biker from the first arrest, and I noticed he was wearing a very similar jacket to Moves'. I knew he was a part of the Outlaw Souls, and that being the case, I could only imagine they were trying to do everything in their power to keep him out of jail.

I fell asleep again right there on the couch, my head filled with more images of Moves, but this time it was in the form of him taking Chalupa's place. I hadn't paid much attention to the man's name before, because at the time it didn't matter, but I was starting to see the same look in that man's eyes that I saw in Moves' every so often. They both looked scared, absolutely terrified that something bad was going to happen, and that didn't scream guilty to me. I've been working the courtroom long enough to be able to pick up on these things, and if it were actually the case that we'd arrested an innocent man, I believed I was capable of doing everything in my power to make sure that he walked.

I'd have to find solid evidence pointing me to the truth before I could ever make a decision like that. I knew that no matter what, the DA was not going to like that one bit. He wanted to crack down on these bikers because he'd been hearing about them for such a long time. On the other hand, I had a duty to uphold justice. Putting innocent people in jail simply because their faces didn't fit was not my reason for becoming a lawyer.

The DA felt it was his duty to keep La Playa and the surrounding areas safe, and he was using me to do it. I was so surprised that he'd even bothered to give me the case when there were so many other people in the office who would've been able to be impartial to the very end, and he was well aware of how attached I could get to such cases.

Maybe that's why he put me on it. Maybe he truly believed that I would stop at nothing to find the truth, and he needed someone like that to head this case. I can see now why Richard was so upset that the DA didn't choose him.

I made my way over to the kitchen to pour myself another cup of coffee, trying to soothe my nerves and calm the uneasiness in my stomach.

The list of questions I had continued to grow, getting longer every day, but I wasn't finding any answers that were going to suffice. I'd been to Ortega's twice. On both occasions, I didn't see a thing that would make me believe that there was criminal activity occurring there, but it was quite possible that either I wasn't looking hard enough, or they were all just good at hiding it from me.

I wondered how many people Moves had told about my job, where I worked, and what to look out for. It made me apprehensive about seeing him again, because I thought that he would be able to see right through me and pick up on my intentions or the feelings that had been front and center ever since our last encounter. I thought back to how he'd helped me at Lily and Bailey's party, and how kind he was when he walked me home. Those were the characteristics of a good man, one that would never stand for something like this, but maybe I was still a bit too naïve when it came to what the Outlaw Souls were really involved in.

I sat back down on the couch with the hot coffee in my hands, hearing the lock turn on the front door, and in strolled Mona, looking as happy as ever. She had a few shopping bags with her. I could tell from her expression that she had already received word from Hawk that they would be seeing each other again, but there was also something pleading in her expression that I couldn't quite understand.

"Someone did a little shopping," I said.

"Oh these few things? I just picked them up on the way home from work, you know because I have a hot date with a really sexy biker guy," she said, giggling.

"Hawk got back to you on that, huh?" I asked, and she nodded.

"I'm really excited, but there's a part of me that's kind of nervous about what I'm getting myself into. I know that you've already warned me about what I could be dealing with, and that's why I have a very strange request for you," she started.

"Oh, no."

"Would you come with me? I know that might sound strange, seeing as how I acted the other night at the bar. I like to think that I'm strong enough to handle this on my own, but the truth is I can't. I need my best friend there, especially because I'm not sure how I feel just yet about everything you've told me. It might be a good chance for us both to start snooping, but I'd just feel better, and a lot more safe if you were there with me," she asked, and I could see just how much she needed me there with her, so I reluctantly nodded.

"All right, I'll come," I said, and she smiled.

"Really? I've been rehearsing those lines all day because I didn't think that you would agree," she said, and I laughed.

"I'll hang around to make sure you're okay. I would never let you go anywhere alone if you weren't fully comfortable. I'll be hiding behind a menu or a laughably conspicuous sunhat," I teased, and she beamed, proceeding to show me all of the outfit choices she'd picked out.

She was genuinely excited, and she was being safe. That was all I ever could've asked for. I knew that there was a part of me that wanted nothing more than to run into Moves, and to get to know him the way we were supposed to before my job got in the way of that. I wanted to spend a bit more time with him, to get him to see that I wasn't all bad. I still had yet to figure out whether they were all innocent in this, because if I ever were to find out that they were truly engaging in criminal activity, I could only imagine that Hawk would've helped.

I looked over at Mona, watching as she tried on those wonderful ensembles, hoping that whatever happened, it wouldn't lead her to getting hurt. The last thing I would want would be for her to be heartbroken because of this. She deserved the world, and I was going to look out for her no matter what happened.

Any time I let my mind wander, I couldn't help but think of the dreams I had of Moves. I couldn't stop focusing on the thought of what his touch must be like, what it must feel like to kiss him, and I was starting to realize that maybe I hadn't been living my life to the fullest like I'd always thought I had.

I was the one that had told Mona that sex was overrated, and there I was dreaming about it like I actually thought it was going to happen. The truth was, I had no idea where Moves and I were going to end up, but if there was one thing I knew for sure, it was that I had to stay focused on bringing the real criminals to justice, no matter who they were. I tried not to think about what that would be like if it were the people I'd started to care about, but I promised myself I would make that decision when the time eventually came.

I feel like I'm nowhere close to finding out what the truth is, but what kind of lawyer would I be if I ignored my gut?

Remembering how many cases I solved off of a single feeling, a single hunch that pointed me in the right direction, I knew I was right. Deep down, I knew that my judgment wasn't clouded to the point where I would side with a criminal blindly without knowing the whole truth. Though, if it did turn out that Moves was involved in things I couldn't wrap my head around, it would be interesting trying to part from it all. I truly felt like I'd gotten to know them all, like I'd had an introduction into their world, and like Mona, I didn't want to leave.

I wished I could've told Mona that I was having feelings about Moves, but I wanted to be sure before I dropped that kind of information on her. She had enough to think about as it was, and the last thing I wanted to do was ruin this moment for her.

I packed away all the case files that were taking up space on the coffee table, trying to relax, and head to bed a little early because I knew that a new day would mean I'd have to continue finding ways to get closer to the Outlaw Souls to gather more information. At least now I had Mona on her way to start dating one of them, so that would at least give me an excuse to hang around without it being too suspicious.

I wondered if I would even run into Moves, if he'd had the same idea as me, and tag along to look out for his friend, even though I was pretty sure that Hawk was capable of taking care of himself. He seemed to be the kind to really take care of them all, to watch out for them when things got hard, and I could tell all of that from the way he helped me, a total stranger on the night we first met. He'd been unlike any guy I'd ever been interested in before, and it made me think that I'd been missing out on what it would be like to find that kind of passionate love that everyone always talked about.

Mona had been talking my ear off about it ever since she convinced me to start dating again, but I never thought that I would've ended up having feelings for a biker, no matter how conflicted they currently made me. There was just no denying that there was a spark between Moves and me. I didn't think I would be able to let it go until I was certain that there was nothing more between us than a bit of a connection that could go one of two ways. Either he was a genuine guy who had no criminal record, or he was someone I had to watch my back around, leaving me more terrified than I was when I first agreed to take this case. I sighed, realizing that once the sun came up, Mona and I would be preparing to head out, and the need to run into Moves again would be clear, but I couldn't tell her that just yet.

I had to be the supportive friend and hang back to make sure that no harm came her way. That was what I promised, and that's exactly what I planned to do.

MOVES

I was riding through a pretty dark part of town, the kind that no one from the Outlaw Souls would ever dare to pass through knowing that Las Balas was roaming around. I felt secure enough to make the drive because I knew that I would be able to shoot myself out of a bad situation if need be, but I was following a hunch that made the need to find out the truth only continue to overwhelm me.

I'd found some evidence that led me to believe that the Las Balas shop had closed, and that they'd had to move to another location to keep their shop open and away from the eyes of the LPPD. If that were the case, then I could only imagine they were the ones framing us and getting Chalupa arrested for grand theft auto when he was nowhere near that car to begin with. It didn't take much for the police to catch on, especially when it came to trying to put people like us behind bars. They were constantly looking for any reason to convict us bikers because they just didn't like having us on the streets.

I didn't care much about what they had planned, because my main focus had shifted from solely making sure that

Chalupa was going to pull through this to finding out if Las Balas was really involved. It could mark the beginning of a war between us gangs, and I was prepared for it to come to that if it was going to finally settle the animosity that had been growing between us for a very long time. I wondered why they would try to do this now, and what their reasons were for framing us when up until recently we were all coexisting quite normally. We stayed out of each other's hair, making sure not to ruffle anyone's feathers while we were just passing through.

I felt the sun beat down on my skin, heating up the leather of my jacket while I revved my engine loudly, letting them know that I was present, and part of the Outlaw Souls. They weren't going to touch me if I didn't pose an immediate threat, and that was exactly what I was counting on. I had to get closer to their operations, and this time I opted to do it alone. I didn't want to peel Hawk away from eating with his girl because it was the happiest he'd been in a very long time, and I'd promised to stop in on my way home to let him know if I found anything else that would point us straight to the people behind this.

I pulled my bike out of sight, knowing that I would have to make the rest of the journey on foot if I was going to break into the Las Balas shop to find out why they were really closed. It wasn't long ago that we were all down at the Blue Dog celebrating the fact that we were rid of the threats presented by Las Balas for the time being, finally able to move on with our lives before being dragged into even more trouble.

That didn't last very long, because here we were again, in the hot seat, trying to find answers that were unfortunately very well hidden. I made sure to stay out of sight using as many back entrances as I could, sneaking through the area as stealthily as possible. There were a few people out roaming the streets, but they didn't seem to be from Las Balas, because I would've been able to tell. They just looked like a bunch of crackheads or prostitutes, out roaming around with no real place to go.

I knew they weren't going to be much of a problem, so I didn't pay them any attention as I tried to figure out how to break the lock on the front of the shop door. I fiddled with it for a few moments, reaching for a loose pipe that was stuck into one of the back dumpsters to help me get it to budge. It took me a little while, but it eventually gave way, and I slid inside before anyone else could see me. I thought for a moment about shooting the lock loose, but I didn't want to bring too much attention to my whereabouts, especially because I could hold off a few rival gang members, but I would be as good as dead if the entirety of Las Balas showed up.

I started looking around to see if they'd left anything behind that would be of use to me or help point me in the direction of where they'd moved the shop to. When I was with Hawk, I found a flyer that said an old abandoned grocery store building was going up for sale, and I could only imagine that they would move to a place like that, somewhere a lot more inward, hiding in plain sight right under the LPPD's nose.

They'd left quite a mess behind, like they truly didn't care about who would find it. I continued looking around, opening up old toolboxes to find torn pieces of clothing, small bags of what appeared to be drugs, and just about everything that made it crystal clear that this was Las Balas' stomping ground. There was nothing besides that flyer I'd found to suggest that they were still using this place, because it was barely operational at this point. I wouldn't have been surprised if they kept it this way so they could use it in their little games, playing cat and mouse with the police, pointing them in the direction of their rival gangs so they would never think to look directly at them.

Their tactics had flair, but it wasn't enough to keep them out of trouble forever. I noticed that the door to the office in the very back of the shop was open, and so I ventured off to see if anything was left behind.

It was eerily quiet as I made my way in, going through the files and ledgers left behind like they weren't really trying to cover their tracks. The place was crawling with evidence that would point to their criminal activity, but the only way I was going to be able to tie it to Las Balas would be for me to find something more incriminating. Although the fact that they'd managed to move their entire shop was enough of a giveaway that told me they had something to hide. I had to figure out what they were trying to cover up, and so I grabbed everything I could, stuffing it all into the bag I'd brought with me, so I could meet up with Hawk and go over the possible leads.

Once I was done, I managed to slip away undetected, getting onto my bike and driving off in the direction of the Blue Dog so I could have a chat with Hawk before he left to spend the rest of the evening with the woman he was seeing. I sighed, remembering the fact that I couldn't even recall the last time I'd felt that way about anyone, and it dawned on me that in everything I'd been doing to protect the Outlaw Souls and keep us out of trouble, I haven't really had much time to date.

I couldn't help but think about Lacey in that moment, reminiscing about how much we'd connected the first time I laid eyes on her at Lily and Bailey's. I just knew that there was something different about her, but I never thought that I would find out she was a prosecuting attorney working for the DA. I still had yet to figure out whether or not she was trying to scope us out and collect evidence on us the same way we were trying to get in order to free Chalupa.

It was a long shot to believe that she was only hanging around us for the sake of her friend, but I wanted to believe that because I could feel myself being drawn to her whenever she was in the room. There was no denying that there was a connection between us, a spark that had been there all along, but I just wasn't sure that getting involved with her would be the best thing for me knowing everything going on.

I had to be fully certain that she didn't have any involvement in Chalupa's case, that she wasn't present to collect evidence, and that there was a part of her that wanted to stick around before I could even see myself with her. But it wasn't going to stop me from having those feelings when I was around her, of wondering what it would be like to feel her skin on mine, to kiss every inch of her. I wanted that more than anything in the world, and I couldn't believe how much it was beginning to consume me.

I was struggling to remain focused on the task at hand whenever the thoughts of Lacey would creep back in when I least expected it, and I knew I had to keep my head on straight if Chalupa had any chance at freedom. I worried that things were only going to get worse, that the fact Las Balas had moved their shop meant that they knew that something was going down or that they were the ones that tipped off the cops so that they would arrest Chalupa in the first place. I could feel my blood boil underneath the surface of my skin whenever I thought about it, wishing I knew the truth by now so I could spend more of my time trying to right the wrongs that had been done to the entire Outlaw Souls community, and we'd be able to move forward. I knew that's what everyone wanted, to feel safe again, to not be on edge, looking over their shoulders any time they traveled outside of our immediate stomping ground.

I wanted to give them that more than anything, to show them that we were strong enough to put forth a united front and take care of our own no matter how difficult things might get. I was going to have to do a much better job of showing them that was a possibility, otherwise I could only imagine they would start to get antsy, to act out of pure impulse, and cause even more problems that we were going to have to fix.

I sighed, riding down to the Blue Dog with the bag slung over my shoulder, a miscellaneous collection of things that could possibly bring us answers if we looked hard enough. It was what I was counting on, because I couldn't imagine we had much more time before Chalupa was going to have to stand in front of a jury and prove that he was innocent for the crime he certainly didn't commit, even though they were probably going to convict him anyway due to the fact he was a biker. It was no secret that the LPPD hated us, and the minute they got the chance to take one of us down, they believed they were one step closer to locking us all up and throwing away the key.

It was in that moment that I had to remember that it was quite possible those were the people who Lacey was most loyal to, and it made me start to wonder whether or not I would be able to part with these feelings welling up inside of me, knowing that they could possibly complicate everything.

I arrived at the Blue Dog, seeing Hawk sitting by the bar all alone, and I glanced down at my wristwatch to see that there was still a bit of time before his date was supposed to show up. I tapped him on the shoulder, nodding my head toward the back office of the Blue Dog where we would be able to talk without everyone trying to figure out what was going on. I needed him to know that the situation was far more complicated than we might have initially realized, and that we were going to have to crack down on Las Balas, finding out whatever we could before things got ugly.

"I was wondering if they'd dragged you away never to be

seen again," he said, rather relieved to see that I was alive and okay.

"I expected them to be where they always were, but remember when I found that flyer outside the shop near where Chalupa was picked up by the police? The one that was talking about the property not too far from there that was up for sale?" I asked, hoping that he would remember.

"Yes, the grocery store that recently went bankrupt."

"Right, well when I made my way over to the Las Balas shop, they had it boarded up. There wasn't one of them in sight, and so I broke into the place looking for more clues, and I brought a few of them with me," I said, handing him the bag for him to look inside.

"Drugs, tools, and car parts?"

"Those look like the kind of parts that would belong to a vehicle similar to the one the police think Chalupa stole?" I asked, and he nodded.

"It seems we might have a few answers waiting for us, but we're going to have to head down to that abandoned grocery store near the railroad tracks if we want to find out for sure. I want to ask you to come with me to check it out, but I know that your date is going to be arriving soon, so I'm going to head this one on my own," I said. He looked at me, guilty for leaving me to walk into Las Balas territory on my own, but I was truly happy for him, and I didn't want to ruin his chance at a fresh start.

"I could call Mona and reschedule. This is important, Moves. I'm afraid to let you walk in there with no protection, or anyone to watch your back," he said, about to pull out his cell phone to call her, but I stopped him.

"You remember why they call me Moves, right? You know that I've supplied each and every one of us with the top of the line artillery that we would need to protect ourselves. I know how to shoot a gun, and I'm not going to get too close if I know the place is swarming with them, I promise," I said, and he nodded.

"If you're sure," he said, not looking entirely convinced.

"Trust me, Hawk. I'm sure," I said, getting ready to leave when we both spotted Mona and Lacey stroll into the Blue Dog. I knew that this was a big moment for Hawk, but part of me still wished that he would've been joining me on this little adventure seeing as it was quite possibly going to get a little messy.

I couldn't help but be distracted by the beautiful Lacey, glancing over at me like she was afraid to say a few words, and I knew why that was. She didn't know if I would want to talk to her, and even after we'd had our last civil conversation, it wasn't enough to convince her that I wanted to be in her company anymore.

I wasn't sure whether it was the fact that I saw Hawk walk off with Mona looking the happiest he'd looked in a very long time, or the fact that I was running solely on adrenaline due to everything that was going on, but I walked over to her with the intention of only saying hello.

The moment I brushed past her, I could feel the sexual tension in the air. It hit me like a truck how much I wanted her, how much I wanted to drag her into the back and kiss every inch of her, to feel her skin brush against mine while I gave her the ride of her life. I'd desired her from the first time I laid eyes on her, and every time since, and this time I just couldn't help but want to be there with her.

I knew that I had other places to be, that I should've been scoping out Las Balas' new stomping ground, but Lacey was just too hard for me to ignore anymore, and I needed to see if this was truly going to go anywhere.

My curiosity got the better of me, and I just couldn't stay away from that beautiful smile of hers. It drew me back in every time I tried to get myself to leave. I knew that it would only cause me trouble if I stuck around, but I had no other choice. It was much too tempting to just walk out of there and pretend like I didn't see her, like I didn't want her right then.

I didn't understand what drew me to her, what made me want to sleep with her so badly, but I wasn't going to give up this time. I wasn't going to allow the fact that she was the prosecuting attorney for the DA scare me away from seeing if we had any real chemistry. I had to know for sure, otherwise it was just going to eat me up inside.

I just can't stay away from you, can I?

LACEY

I didn't expect to feel this way when I saw him again. I knew that the chemistry between us existed, but I didn't think that I would be having trouble catching my breath around him. He looked like he was in a rush, but now he doesn't seem like he wants to leave, and I have to wonder, is that because of me?

Glancing toward the back of the Blue Dog, I could see that Hawk and Mona were enjoying their evening, laughing, smiling, and having a great time. It was much more surreal to see their connection in person, to understand why she'd been so nervous around Hawk, because I was starting to feel the same way about Moves.

He brought two beers over to the small table in the back that I'd been sitting at, trying to stay out of sight so I didn't make the two lovebirds uncomfortable.

"I didn't expect to see you here," he said, and I shrugged, nodding my head over in the direction of Hawk and Mona, watching him quickly put the pieces together.

"Ah, so you're here to make sure that Hawk doesn't try any funny business," he said, and I motioned for him to join me.

"Oh, they've already made it to funny business, but I'm sure he probably filled you in on that one already," I said, and he chuckled, handing me the cold beer. I sipped it lightly, my heart beating loudly in my chest every time I looked at him. I was secretly really glad to see him, because I knew how truly boring my evening was going to be if he didn't show up. I had a million questions running through my mind to ask him, but the last thing I wanted to do was scare him off again.

I was sure that he was still trying to process the fact that I was a lawyer, one that was working in the very place that would be prosecuting a friend of his, but I knew that it was the wrong time to be questioning him about those things.

Now that I was able to get a good look at him, I noticed how tired he looked, how the bags under his eyes remained prevalent, though it didn't take away from how incredibly attractive and strong he was.

He removed his leather jacket, and I got a good look at those strong arms of his in the tight black T-shirt he was wearing. I immediately felt myself get hot, my cheeks began to flush, and I turned straight to the beer to cool me down and take my mind off of it.

You are here to look after Mona and make sure that she's okay. Though she looks just fine, and to be quite honest, I've never felt a rush quite like this before.

I gazed into Moves' eyes, wondering what must be going through his mind right then.

"You're quite the supportive friend coming all the way out here just to watch over Mona," he said, sipping on his beer.

"Well, you looked like you were in a rush, but you decided to stay too, so I assume you're also looking out for your friend," I said, and he shook his head.

"Actually, I stayed to talk to you. I know that we haven't exactly had the best time lately, but I want to apologize for my behavior. I just have a lot going on right now, and it hasn't exactly made me the kindest person to be around," he confessed.

I appreciated the sentiment even though I had an inkling why he was so distressed, but I decided to keep my mouth shut.

"It's all right, Moves. I'm just glad that we're able to talk now. Trust me when I say, I've been trying to get out of my head lately too. All I want is to let loose a little and do something for me, something I can enjoy again, but I've been so caught up that I just haven't been able to," I confessed, realizing that it was much easier than I thought to tell him exactly how I felt.

"Have you ever taken a ride on the back of a motorcycle?" he asked, genuinely curious, and I shook my head. Ever since I found out that they were bikers, I'd thought about it from time to time, wondering what it would be like to feel the wind in my hair, to experience the open road without anyone trying to stop us.

"I unfortunately have not, but seeing as everyone around here owns one, I'm sure that it must be quite the experience," I teased, and he immediately got up from his chair, outstretching his hand for me to take it, and I did.

I didn't know what came over me, but I was falling for the allure of Moves, and how incredibly freeing it felt to be with him. I wanted to experience everything that he had to offer, however he wished to do so.

We bid goodbye to Hawk and Mona, and he led me out of the Blue Dog. Mona glanced back at me as we left, winking when she picked up on the fact that I was having a bit of an experience on my own. He handed me a helmet, and I struggled to put it on, because I had absolutely no idea what I was doing. He chuckled, helping me adjust it so it wouldn't fall right off my head, and then he got onto the bike and started up the engine.

"Are you ready?" he asked.

"Are you sure this is okay? I don't know if we should just leave, I mean—"

"Hey, Lacey. Weren't you the one that said you wanted to live a little? I suggest you hold on tight because it's going to be one hell of a ride," he said, and I hopped onto the back, wrapping my arms around his torso, holding on as tightly as I possibly could.

I couldn't deny that it felt incredible to be that close to him, to feel the warmth emanating through his T-shirt while he took off. I let out a little scream, because I didn't expect it to go that fast that quickly, and it wasn't long before we were zipping down the road so fast that I truly couldn't believe it. At first I was scared, worried that I was going to fall off or hurt myself, but I eventually let it all go.

There was a part of me that truly believed Moves would never hurt me, that he would never do anything to put me in immediate danger, and that alone made me feel safe. I was able to let go of all my worries, everything that had been bottled up inside of me for days waiting to be let out. I felt freer than I'd ever felt in my entire life, and I was out on the road with a hot biker guy who I certainly wanted to sleep with.

I didn't know what came over me, or how the adrenaline found its way into my veins, but I was on a high I'd never been on before. When I let out a scream of excitement, I could see Moves turn his head back and smile at me, and we both shared that moment together, wondering where it was going to lead.

I wanted to ask him where we were going, if it was safe there, and if we were even allowed to be out around these parts, and then I realized that I was getting into my head again. I decided to let Moves take the wheel entirely, to lead me wherever he wanted to take me, because I wasn't quite sure I was ever going to get an opportunity like that again.

He made me feel incredible, and I couldn't explain the excitement that erupted through me, waiting for him to take the next turn, speeding down the highway like he owned the road. It was absolutely mind-blowing, and when he eventually rode out to the beach, slowing down around the pier, I realized that I was sad that we were stopping.

The beach looked absolutely beautiful at this time of the night. It was much cooler out than I expected, and Moves led me down to where the waves were coming in, while I took off my shoes to feel the sand between my toes, and the coolness of the water washed over my feet.

"That was amazing. I don't think I'd ever felt anything like that before," I confessed, and he looked quite pleased with himself. It was one of the only times I'd seen a genuine smile on his face. It made me feel good, like we were really having a moment together, but that only left me even more conflicted.

I didn't want to think about the fact that my feelings for Moves were growing by the minute, especially if there was the chance that he didn't feel the same way about me, but I had to ignore it. I ignored the worry because I was so drawn to him in that moment that I could do just about anything. I felt invincible around him, like I possessed this unimaginable kind of strength, and I wanted to go for a ride all over again, but he had something completely different in mind.

"You know, there was a part of me that didn't think you would actually enjoy it. You don't seem like the type," he said, and I stared at him blankly, wondering if there was any truth to his words.

"To be honest, I didn't think I was the type to enjoy it either, but apparently you've unlocked an entirely different side to me that I didn't even know existed," I said, doing a light twirl, feeling the water swish beneath my feet while I enjoyed the calm, beautiful night.

"You look cold. I left my jacket back at the Blue Dog, but I think we can find some wood around here to build a fire," he said, and I smiled, knowing that would be wonderful. I helped him look, gathering a few twigs and other miscellaneous items that would provide a nice flame while I watched him go to work, getting it to light, and I reached out to feel the warmth on my hands. He sat down next to me, and I could feel my heart start to beat loudly in my chest again, reminding me of just how nervous I was around him, especially with him being so close to me.

I wanted him to kiss me, I wanted him to touch every inch of me, and I couldn't understand why. I'd never felt that way about a guy before, and I was always convinced that it was just because up until this point I'd never been interested in anything more than my job.

It was then that I realized just how much of life I'd been missing out on, and that I needed to get out of my head long enough to enjoy this moment, because there was always the chance I would never get to feel this way again. I still didn't know what Moves' intentions were, or what the Outlaw Souls were truly involved in, but right then I wanted to forget all of my inhibitions and just enjoy that moment with him. He glanced over at me, his eyes lowering to my lips the way they had before I had blurted out to him that I was a lawyer, and this time, he caressed my cheek, pressing his lips up against mine.

That very kiss ignited something inside of me that I didn't understand, a need, an urge to feel every inch of him the way I had in that dream a few days ago.

I let his hands travel down my body, and with every brush of his fingertips, I could feel the satisfying tingle, wondering what he was going to do next. He pulled down the strap of my shirt, kissing down my neck to the very top of my shoulders, and I caressed his head, running my fingers through his hair while his kisses journeyed a bit lower.

"Is this all right?" he whispered in my ear, and I nodded. I felt him help me out of my jeans, while I pulled my shirt up over my head. There I was, lying on his T-shirt and gazing up at him while he took in every inch of my nearly naked body. He slipped out of his jeans, spreading my legs so he could get between them, while I bit my lip, already wetter than I'd ever been before. My mind and heart was racing with the possibilities, with what I was about to feel, because I already knew that it was going to be unlike anything I'd ever experienced.

Moves had a way of captivating me like no other man did, and it wasn't until that very moment that I realized I wanted every inch of him inside of me. He unhooked my bra, all while his lips stayed passionately pressed up against mine, his tongue playfully reaching into my mouth while I lay back. Then I felt his lips enclose around my nipple, biting down ever so softly.

I looked down to see his hard erection piercing through his boxers, and I ran my hands along the shaft, waiting for him to pull it out and slip inside of me. I took a deep breath, and he pulled his boxers down, sliding his dick deep inside my pussy while my entire body erupted with an immense amount of pleasure.

Our bodies heated up, and I could feel him work up a sweat while he thrust deep inside me. I let out a moan. It was so good that I felt my eyes begin to roll to the back of my head, and he ran his hands through my hair, yanking on it while he rammed every inch of himself deeper and deeper inside of me until I came. I was on the verge of an orgasm right then, realizing that I had been wrong about sex all along, that I had been missing out all this time trying to convince myself that no one would ever be able to make me feel this way.

Moves changed that. He took care of my body, giving me that raw, real ride of my life that he'd promised.

He held me there while we curled up on top of the pile of clothes, cuddling by the fire, while I fell asleep right there in his arms. I felt so good, so protected, so safe and happy when I was with him, even though I was still rather confused on what exactly this meant for us.

I was falling asleep thinking that it could've just been a hookup to him, that he might not have felt anything for me at all, and I knew that I couldn't allow myself to get too attached because I was just going to end up getting hurt.

As amazing as it was, I had to protect myself and my heart from shattering, just in case he really didn't feel much of anything for me. I slept there with him comfortably, waking up to the steady stream of sunlight behind my eyelids when I heard a voice over me that certainly didn't belong to Moves.

When I finally awoke, I looked up to see a man standing over me with the biggest grin on his face, and that's when I realized I wasn't wearing much of anything.

"Ma'am, are you okay?" he asked, and I realized that he was a lifeguard stationed there, probably just starting his shift when he saw me completely knocked out on the beach, but Moves was nowhere to be found.

"Yes, um I suppose I just fell asleep, thank you," I said, and he walked away while I got dressed into the clothes I'd been wearing earlier. Hearing my phone ring in my jeans, I fished it out to answer it.

"Hello?"

"Hi, this is your Uber. I'm waiting down by the pier," said the unknown caller, and I realized that Moves had called me a ride home instead of taking me himself.

How absolutely classy of him.

I told the Uber driver that I was only going to be a few minutes. I was fuming, wondering why Moves would've left without saying goodbye, or why he wouldn't have at least given me the courtesy of waking me before he took off.

I had to remember what I was thinking about before I fell asleep, because if it was true that this was just another hookup to him, then that meant he probably did this sort of thing all the time. It didn't make me feel any better, and I got into the back of my Uber feeling quite terrible that I let it get to this point.

I couldn't deny that I had feelings for Moves, but now I was fairly sure that he didn't feel the same way about me. For a moment there, I thought I had been right about him, judging from the way he kissed me, from the way he always seemed to take care of me, but I supposed I'd just been reading a little too much into it. I had to dial it back, find something else to fixate on, because it seemed that Moves had already moved on.

MOVES

Why did I run? Why did I just leave her there like that?

I felt guilty for leaving without saying another word. I could've only imagined how furious she would've been when she woke up, wondering whether last night had been a mistake, but it scared me more than I would've admitted.

I'd wanted to sleep with her for a very long time, but I didn't think that once I did, I would start having any feelings for her. They crept in when I least expected it, and I found myself falling for her right then, but I knew that was just going to complicate things.

Now, I was sure that I had blown it, because I would have to be a fool to think that she was going to take me back after I'd just abandoned her on the beach after sleeping with her.

I kept going back to the moment where I'd woken up cuddled up next to her, realizing that I felt more than just the satisfaction of sleeping with a gorgeous girl. The feelings I had inside of me were ones I simply couldn't understand, and I'd never felt that way about anyone before in my life. I didn't know how to process it all, I didn't know if it even made sense knowing where she worked and how complicated our relationship was.

I wished I could've gone back, slept with her, and woken up to kiss her the way I wanted to. I ran because I was afraid, I was afraid to let myself feel something other than the need to protect the Outlaw Souls. I didn't think I had it in me to care about anyone else other than the people that have become family over the years, but I soon realized that I was wrong.

I was falling hard for Lacey, and it hurt me even more to know that she probably wasn't going to want to see me after the stunt I had pulled. I drove back home just after sunrise that morning, trying to forget the entire occurrence, to regain the focus I needed to help the Outlaw Souls and help Chalupa finally have his freedom. It was much easier said than done, though.

Any time I closed my eyes, even if it was just for a split second, I remembered what it was like to have my hands all over her body. I remembered what it felt like to kiss her, to hold her close, and it was amazing to feel that she was mine, even if it was only for that evening.

I realized that I might not ever know how she truly felt about me because I'd ruined everything—just like I did every other relationship I'd ever been in.

I didn't give myself the chance to see where it was going, and I had a feeling I was going to regret that for the rest of my life, unless I could convince Lacey that I wasn't that bad a guy.

I could imagine that she was going to head home fuming, ready to tell Mona about the wonderful night she'd had only to follow it up with the terrible morning, remembering that I was just as bad as she initially thought. I didn't want her to hate me, I didn't want her to shut me out completely, but I didn't know how else to process what I was feeling. They were emotions that were entirely foreign to me, and I had to figure them out before I gave her false hope.

It was quite clear that we shared a connection, but I wondered if that truly meant that we were ever going to end up together.

There were so many things standing between us, keeping us from being able to explore each other, because we both had responsibilities that heavily contrasted each other.

My first loyalty was to the Outlaw Souls, and I was sure that her loyalty was to her job. I didn't know how we were ever going to be able to make that work even if we tried, especially if she really was involved with Chalupa's case.

I didn't think that anyone from the Outlaw Souls would be okay with that, and I wasn't sure that I would, but I wasn't going to be able to deny how I felt forever.

Lacey, what have you done to me?

I had been so clear headed before I met her, able to focus solely on trying to get Chalupa the freedom he so rightfully deserved. Though I also had to acknowledge just how sad my life had been before I met her, because she brought a different kind of light to my life that I didn't expect.

I never smiled as much when I wasn't around her, I never felt challenged by anyone like her before, and those were all things that made me want to fight for her, even though there was a part of me that felt like no matter what I did, it was just destined to end badly.

I knew I was being hard on her, criticizing her for working for the DA even though we were living in two completely different worlds, but I didn't know how to mesh them even if I wanted to.

I could've only hoped that I was going to figure out how to do that soon, otherwise I was going to have the guilt of not knowing what we could've been eat away at me. That was going to be far worse than the realization that we were never going to work out. I had to know for sure if she and I were meant to be, if there was any way we could get past everything that had been happening and eventually find our way back to each other.

That is, if she can even find it in her heart to forgive me.

I had to focus on the task at hand, because I finally had reason to believe that Las Balas were the ones behind Chalupa's arrest, and I was that much closer to unraveling the mystery for myself. I still decided to go at it alone, because it was going to be much easier for me to sneak around by myself than to have Hawk with me, even though there was always the possibility that I was going to need backup.

I got on my bike, heading down to the new location of the Las Balas shop to see if I could find out anything else that would finally bring this case to a close.

I had to make sure to stay out of sight because the last thing I needed was for them to catch me there. I could only imagine what they would do if they managed to subdue me.

We'd had run-ins with them before, but it was never like this. I was never trying to find solid evidence as to why they would retaliate like this when we'd done nothing to harm them.

We'd always managed to stay in our lane, and for the most part they'd been incredibly quiet over the last few months. I was starting to think that they weren't going to be much of a problem anymore until Chalupa called me from the station.

Now I wanted to fight back with a vengeance, enact my revenge on them the very way they'd tried to set us up and wipe us out. I could feel in my gut that we were getting closer, that I was finally going to have the answers to those questions that had been eating away at my brain.

I made sure to pull up a bit of a distance away from the railroad tracks, trying to see what I could from behind their shop. There were Las Balas crawling everywhere, and they all looked rather smug, as though something was about to go down. I had a sick feeling in the pit of my stomach, like there was something going on here that was far more dangerous than any of us realized, and so I continued to inch closer.

I hid behind the surrounding buildings, trying to get as close as possible without anyone seeing me, feeling for my gun in its holster at my back to make sure that I could shoot my way out if I absolutely had to.

I gulped, peeking my head around the corner to see a few Las Balas members meet a car that certainly didn't look like it belonged there. It was a black sedan, the kind that was used by the police when they were trying to go undercover. I kept watching as the car slowly pulled into their shop, and I peered through the dirty window to see who was going to get out of it.

There is no way that Las Balas could've teamed up with the police, could there?

If that was the case, we were going to have much more of a problem than I initially realized.

I kept watching while the car slowly came to a stop, and out of the driver's seat came the last person that I ever expected to see on Las Balas ground.

The DA is involved with this?

For a moment I thought that maybe he was trying to scope things out for himself, pretending to go undercover to find out more about what their operations were like, but that just didn't seem to be the case.

I pulled out my cell phone and set it to video mode. I recorded as the doors to the office swung open to reveal the leader of the Las Balas, El Diablo. I watched the two of them interact, looking as though they were having a pleasant conversation, and the more I looked on, the angrier I became.

The DA is the one trying to silence the Outlaw Souls because he's making a deal with El Diablo? What could he DA possibly be bribed with to ignore his responsibilities, ignore the law for the sake of letting them walk?

I heard footsteps approach me, so I ducked down behind one of the dumpsters in the back while I watched two of the men walk out to light up a cigarette.

It took them a while to leave, but out of the corner of my eye, I could've sworn I saw the black sedan leave, and that's when I knew that we had a much bigger problem on our hands than any of us could've guessed.

I thought about what to do, about how we were going to get out of this mess knowing that the most powerful man around was in Las Balas' pockets. It didn't make any sense, and I wondered what they'd promised him to get that sort of response.

El Diablo was the one that sent the DA after us, planting false evidence to make the arrest look legit even though they had nothing on which to convict Chalupa. I was starting to worry, because I didn't know how we were going to prove Chalupa's innocence to the people that mattered knowing that the DA was involved in all of this. He was the last person I expected to be dirty, but now I had access to information I was going to have to act on fast, otherwise I knew it would be the end of the Outlaw Souls.

I managed to take a blurry video of the exchange, but I didn't even know if that sort of thing would be admissible in court.

I didn't know the first thing about how any of this worked, and I wondered who was going to be able to help me see this through. Not only did I have Las Balas to worry about, but now I had to find a way to expose the DA with nothing but a little video that might or might not be the answer we'd been looking for.

I was overwhelmed with stress, making my way back to

my bike so I could take off in the direction of Hawk's place, because I needed some advice on how to move forward with this. I knew if I called a meeting with the rest of the Outlaw Souls, the first thing any of them were going to want to do would be to storm Las Balas' new shop and take as many of them out as possible. That was just going to give the police more reason to convict us all, and I wasn't going to let anyone go down for this, now knowing the truth.

I arrived at Hawk's house not long after. He opened up the door with a beer in his hand, looking as chipper as ever. The moment he got a good look at the expression on my face, he knew there was trouble.

I finally had solid evidence to prove that the DA was involved, that El Diablo had been the one orchestrating this whole thing from the very beginning, but it was only going to make things much more difficult to prove. I was sure that the DA was no stranger to tampering with evidence, and I knew that if I let this video get into the wrong hands, it was going to be lost before anyone could have the chance to see it. I just couldn't let that happen, and so I had to make sure that no one else knew about its existence.

"What is it, Moves?"

"Open up, I have something I need to show you," I said, and he unlocked the screen door, letting me inside. I collapsed onto his couch, running my palm along my face out of pure frustration.

"I made a little visit to Las Balas' new shop, trying to see if there was anything there that could point us to the truth and something that would lead to Chalupa's freedom, but what I saw instead made me wonder if we're ever going to get out of this," I said, pulling out my cell phone and handing it to Hawk with the video clearly displayed so he could see for himself.

"How the hell is this even possible? What would the DA

want that El Diablo could give him?" Hawk asked, and I wished I had any of those answers.

"I have no idea, but something tells me this has been in the works for quite some time, and that means we're going to have much more trouble on our hands than I initially realized," I confessed, and Hawk shook his head, unable to believe that this was the evidence I'd found.

"What are we going to do? I'm sure the DA already has a plan in place, a viable alibi that would keep him from ever being caught."

"Videos and timestamps don't lie, unfortunately. If this got into the right hands and it was verified, then we would be able to prove that this entire case has been dirty from the very beginning," I said.

"And if it gets into the wrong hands then there just won't be any saving Chalupa or the rest of us, will there?" I shook my head.

"We just have to make sure that doesn't happen, so don't tell anyone about the video, because I have yet to figure out who I can trust to use this to the best of our advantage. It's a smoking gun if we figure out how to use it properly, I just don't know who to turn to right now." He looked at me like I already knew who I should be talking to about this, but I shook my head, realizing that it could very well be a terrible idea.

"You're gonna have to tell Lacey about this. If there's one thing I know about that girl it's that she would do anything for the truth, and she was always going to stand up for what was right," he said, and even though I agreed with him I was worried that she just wasn't going to want to help.

"As much as that may be true, I don't even think she wants to see me right now. I don't even think she would hear me out after what I did."

He glared at me, trying to figure out what I could've possibly done.

"What did you do, Moves?"

"I slept with her and then I left her right as the sun came up, because for the first time in my entire life, I felt something. I went running scared because I had no idea how to deal with any of those emotions, and now she has every right to hate me. How am I going to get her to help us now?" I asked, and he looked at me like I already knew the answer to that question.

Hawk gave me a stern look. "You're going to have to fix things with her, and you're going to have to get her on our side because I believe that's the only chance we have of seeing this through."

"I'll try my best, but what if she doesn't want to see me?"

"Then you're going to have to own up to those emotions that scared you and finally tell her how you feel."

I knew he had a point, but I'd never been the kind of person that would be good in a relationship, much less one with a lawyer. There was no way that I could ever be good enough for a woman like Lacey, and I felt like she was going to leave me in the dust when she realized that she could have anyone she wanted. She seemed like the type to fall for the rich, notable lawyers, not a biker who was struggling to make his way every day. I had to at least tell her the truth. After what I'd done, I at least owed her that.

LACEY

I couldn't help but feel the hurt creep back in every time I closed my eyes, standing under the shower head in my bathroom trying to wash the sand and the memories away. I felt the warmth encapsulate me, allowing me to dive into my feelings without the worry that Mona was going to rush in asking if I was okay.

I wanted to set aside my feelings, to remember that it was probably all just a hookup to him, and that he didn't feel things the way I did. I felt like it was my own fault for getting involved with a biker, without ever asking him if he'd felt what I had been feeling the last few weeks, and I got involved looking for a bit of adventure, but all I got was hurt.

I tried to forget the memory of last night, tried to set aside the fact that Moves probably only ever saw me as a conquest, someone that he wanted to sleep with, but he didn't care much about what happened after that. It was exactly the kind of thing that I'd been afraid of, and it was what had held me back so long when it came to even entertaining the idea.

I hoped that it was just one big misunderstanding, that he

was going to find his way back into my life and make it up to me for leaving without so much as saying goodbye. If I had only known what I was getting myself into, I probably would've convinced myself to stay away, to protect my heart, because now it was absolutely shattered.

I got out of the shower, wrapped my body in a towel, and wiped off the mirror so I could get a good look at my sullen reflection. I closed my eyes, trying to take a deep breath, but all I could focus on was how incredible Moves' touch had been, how amazing it felt to have him hover over me, kiss every inch of my body, and make me feel like no one ever had before.

I knew that I had to work on forgetting all of that, otherwise I was just going to end up hurting myself time and time again, while he was out there getting back to a sense of normalcy in his life. I wasn't sure that I was ever going to have that again, because I'd gotten so caught up in everything with the Outlaw Souls that I had no evidence to show the DA, and I could only imagine that my career was going to take a big hit after this one. I'd never been more disappointed in myself than I was right now, and I would've done anything to get that time back.

I sighed, slipping into a pair of sweats, not even in the mood to look over my case files again, because in my heart I already knew that Ortega's was clean and there was no criminal activity happening there. I didn't know how else to tell the DA that there just wasn't anything to find, especially because he was so convinced that there was, but now I was starting to feel like he was going to take it out on me.

I still wondered why I'd been chosen for the job, what that spiel the DA gave me at the very start of all of this really meant, because I was starting to wonder whether someone else would've been able to do a much better job than I ever could. I knew that Richard wouldn't have found himself getting caught up in the lives of these people, people he barely knew.

I realized that I barely knew them either, and even though I was trying everything in my power to get to know them, to understand how their world worked, it was much harder than I could've ever imagined.

It was because of Moves that I'd started to change my mind, and for a moment he'd made me believe that there was something more to him than just being a biker. I'd heard stories and rumors all my life about how they operated, about their disregard for basic human connections, and I was starting to think that Moves was just another one of them. I wondered what he really wanted to get out of life, and for a moment I began to think that there was a possibility he just didn't know how to face his emotions like the rest of us did.

I wanted to believe that there was a part of him that felt something other than my body last night, that there was a part of him that cared for me, but at this point, I had a feeling that was just wishful thinking.

I headed out into the kitchen to fix myself something to eat, and I had the house to myself for a little while until Mona got home from work. I was supposed to be out finding incriminating evidence, but after last night I just couldn't seem to think straight anymore. It was all too much for me to handle, and I was starting to think that maybe it was time I threw in the towel on this one.

The day passed by incredibly quickly, and it wasn't long before I heard the front door unlock, revealing a giddy Mona, who wore the happiest expression on her face until she got one good look at how I was doing. She stopped right in her tracks, tossing her things onto the floor and rushed over to me to ask what was wrong.

"Lacey? Are you okay?" she asked, but she knew the answer to that question. I couldn't remember the last time I had been this distraught, and it made me feel terrible that I couldn't pull it together even though I knew I should've known better.

"I slept with Moves, Mona."

"Oh, I knew that you two had quite the connection, but I didn't think..."

"And when I woke up this morning, he was gone. He didn't tell me that he was leaving, and I'm starting to think that I wasn't even owed an explanation, but I guess that's what I deserve for getting involved with someone like him." I glanced down at the floor while Mona threw her hands around me, pulling me in for a tight embrace to make me feel a little better.

"I am going to find him, and I'm going to kill him for this," she said.

"No, it's my fault. I should've known we were just hooking up, but there was something about all of it that felt different, that made me believe even if just for a second that he actually cared about me," I confessed, and she nodded.

"Let me get in touch with Hawk and see what he can do," she said, and I wanted to stop her, but I knew she was going to do everything in her power to crack down on Moves for hurting me, even if I should've been more aware of what was going on.

My heart hurt more than it had in a very long time, and I didn't know how to make any of it feel better.

I spent the afternoon curled up on the couch, trying to calm my nerves while Mona brought me over a cup of tea. She stayed with me to watch a movie so I could try to get my mind off of things, but it didn't help. I felt like a failure in both my budding relationship and my job. I didn't know how I was going to face the DA without so much as a sliver of evidence that could tie Ortega's to the chop shop allegations, and I was going to have to watch while he told me exactly why he put me on the job, possibly firing me for not being able to do the one thing he asked of me.

I was feeling so down about everything that happened, but it felt good to let it out for a little while. Mona dragged me to bed, tossing the covers over my legs so I could try to get some sleep, and I thanked her for always being there for me. There wasn't a moment that I didn't appreciate having her around, and it was now that I realized that I needed her more than ever.

I was just about to drift off to sleep when I heard my cell phone buzz on my nightstand. I truly wasn't in the mood to talk to anyone, so I let it ring, waiting for it to cut out, but the minute it did, it started to ring again. I realized that if I didn't answer, whoever was calling just wasn't going to give up, so I looked at the number. I didn't recognize it, but I answered anyway.

"Hello?"

"Lacey? This is Moves," he said, and just like that my heart sank into my stomach.

"What do you want?" I asked, trying to lessen my firm tone, but I just couldn't help myself.

"I know that I'm probably the last person that you want to hear from right now, but there's something I need to show you, and it's urgent. I'm going to need you to meet me at the pier," he said, and he sounded serious, but I really wasn't in the mood to engage with any of this, especially after leaving me at the pier alone that very morning.

"I think that whatever it is, Moves, you're probably fully capable of handling it on your own. Okay? I don't want to meet you at the pier when that was the very place I had to leave from this morning, all alone I might add," I said, sounding as bitter as I felt, and I could tell that he was desperate because he was still hanging on.

It was at that moment that I realized whatever he was

going to tell me was of the utmost importance, and if I didn't meet him, I was probably never going to know what he had to say.

"Lacey, please. I know that I messed things up between us, but I promise that I will explain everything once you get here. This unfortunately isn't about us, and I'm going to need you to trust me on this," he said, and I could hear it in his voice that he was being genuine. I tossed the covers from my legs, pulling out a few pieces of clothes to change into, and decided that there was no better time than the present to figure out what he was talking about.

"Fine, I'll be there."

I hoped that I wasn't going to regret meeting up with Moves, especially knowing that he was going to try to fix things any way he knew how, but I wasn't sure I wanted to hear any of those words from him. I didn't know what I wanted or if I even cared for him. I wished he could have been more like Hawk.

I decided not to hold out hope, because there was a chance that he wasn't going to tell me what I wanted to hear anyway.

MOVES

Can I trust her with this? How will I know for sure if this is going to be the right thing to do? What if I show her this video and she goes running back to the DA to tell him what's been going on? I know she's not going to do that, but the thought still scares me, especially after I hurt her so badly.

I was trying to tell myself that everything was going to be okay, that we were finally closer to getting to the bottom of this, but we needed someone on the inside that would be able to help us.

The DA had El Diablo doing anything he asked, and the thought of that made me sick, because after everything we'd done to avoid the LPPD over the years, they came knocking on our door to take one of ours away on account of a bribe. That was the dirtiest thing I'd ever heard, and I wanted nothing more than to prove to everyone that we weren't the ones that deserved to be behind bars right now. We deserved better than that, and I could only hope that Lacey was going to help us expose the DA for being nothing more than a dirty cop with a superiority complex.

He was abusing his power, siding with the people who

would do anything to maintain their fortune, to dabble in the darkest parts of what this life is truly like. It was quite tragic to see, because I knew what it was like to be abused, to be thrown around like my life meant nothing, and that was exactly what Las Balas did to innocent people on a daily basis.

I knew how terrible their practices were, and that the only thing they ever cared about was making more money. They'd repeatedly thrown their own under the bus for the sake of making more cold, hard cash, and the thought of that made my blood boil. I couldn't imagine doing that to anyone from the Outlaw Souls, no matter how much they might have angered me, because that was simply not the kind of people we were. We cared about our own, and we protected our own before anyone else.

Now, I had to trust someone who had every right to hate me, to help protect us, because I feared that if we waited any longer, the deal was going to go through and they were going to start rounding us up before we had the chance to do anything about it.

I worried about what that moment would be like, about how terrified they'd all be to know that they never stood a chance because the DA had already signed a deal that sealed every single one of their fates. They were all going to run scared, and those who were taken first might have been persuaded to talk. That was not something I could allow to happen, and I was going to do everything in my power to make sure that the DA paid for trying to take us down.

Lacey had goodness in her heart, but I didn't want her to act on impulse, because she truly hated my guts at this time, and understandably so. I didn't want her to make her decision solely based on the fact that I was a terrible human being who didn't know the first thing about love, and I had to show her that I hadn't left because I didn't care; I left because I was afraid of letting those feelings consume me.

I wanted to be there for her, I wanted to be everything she could ever need, but I was afraid that if I gave in entirely, I wasn't going to be the same person anymore. I didn't know how I was going to play the role of a neutral enforcer when all I would ever care about would be protecting Lacey, because I was falling in love with her. There was no point in denying it any longer.

I waited there under the moonlight for her to come back, to help me. I know I didn't deserve to have her love after what I'd done, but I hoped that she would be able to forgive me for my terrible behavior and help us get out of this mess once and for all.

Looking out onto the beach, I remembered how wonderful it was to hold her in my arms, to feel a sense of calm and contentment wash over me like it was the very first time I'd ever felt that way. I never wanted to leave that moment, much less abandon her on the beach where she was left to believe that I didn't care about her.

I promised myself that I wouldn't even bother to ask her to help until I could show her how I really felt, because it was only then that she was going to have the peace of mind she needed to be able to help us see this through.

I'm falling in love with you, Lacey, and I did everything I could possibly do to mess that up. I don't know how you're going to find it in your heart to forgive me, but I just hope that you do.

Bracing against the ledge of the pier, staring down into the bleak, dark waters below, I knew that there was still hope that we could fix this, that we could get Chalupa out of this mess, and finally bring the Outlaw Souls some comfort knowing this wasn't ever going to happen again.

I waited for what felt like ages, worried that she was going to change her mind and not bother to show up at all, and I was just about to turn around to leave when I saw a car pull up at the end of the pier and out she came. She walked down to where I was standing looking as beautiful as ever, like I'd just dragged her out of bed to meet me, but I knew this couldn't wait.

"I'm here, now what do you want?" she asked, angrily.

"Let me just start off by saying that you have every right to be angry with me, Lacey. I know what I did was wrong, and I know it probably solidified the perception you have of me, making you think that I'm some heartless guy that could just go around leading women on only to sleep with them, but that's simply not the truth. I didn't leave you this morning because I didn't feel anything for you. I left because I felt too much."

She stared at me blankly, trying to figure out what I was saying.

"So what you're telling me is that you're a coward who has an inability to face his feelings?" Lacey pursed her lips and looked away, her arms tightly folded across her chest.

"That's exactly what I am, and I'm going to spend the rest of my life making it up to you, Lacey, because I don't want to lose you. I don't want to lose what we have together. You've come into my life and changed it in ways I never even realized until I had the chance to kiss you, to take you into my arms, and I threw that all away because I was afraid. I know that you might not find it in your heart to forgive me right now, but that's okay. I will wait, and I will keep trying."

"Have you any idea how it felt to be left like that, on the beach, practically naked to be woken up by a lifeguard?" Lacey turned away and began pacing up and down. "Oh, but you were good enough to call Uber and have them pick me up." She pointed her finger to where the cab had been parked.

"Yes, I realize how bad that must seem." It never occurred to me just how humiliated she must have felt. "Please, Lacey, believe me when I say I am truly sorry. I panicked, and yes, I am a coward when it comes to emotions, but I am working on that." I looked into her eyes for any glimmer of hope, but just saw anger.

I couldn't wait any longer. I had to confront her with the other reason I wanted to see her out here tonight.

"Lacey, I'd be lying if I said that was the only reason I called you." She looked at me, shocked, confused, possibly intrigued. I couldn't really tell, but I had to press on. I couldn't turn back now.

I hesitated for a moment, thinking that it was quite possible that she might run with this right back to the DA, protecting him even though he was the one at fault, but I had to trust her. I had to trust her because even though she was a prosecuting attorney, she'd never done anything to hurt me.

Even if she had set out to collect information on us, to gather as much evidence as possible, she quickly learned that there simply wasn't any to be found. I knew that was probably going to strike a rather large nerve with the DA because he probably sent Lacey out with the intention of finding something incriminating enough to take us down while Las Balas continued to get their way.

I took a deep breath, pulled out my phone, and scrolled through until I found the video. I put it into her hands, watching her facial expressions while she wondered for a moment what she was looking at, and the minute she recognized the DA's face, her entire expression dropped. She blinked heavily, trying to figure out if what she was watching had been real, and when she glanced back up at me, I nodded, letting her know that I was the one that took the video in the first place.

"This can't be real." She shook her head as if that would make it untrue. "There is no way in hell that he would get involved with something like this. Is this the other guy that you were telling me about, El Diablo?"

I nodded.

"Is this some kind of sick and twisted way to use me against the DA?" she asked, and I knew that she was going to have a considerable amount of doubt, but I just had to make sure that she was able to see the truth before it was too late.

"Lacey, I was there. I saw this exchange happen with my very own eyes. I know that it's a lot for you to take in, but it is certainly happening right under all of our noses. I know what your involvement at the DA's office is like, and I know where your loyalty lies, but I brought this to you because the DA is helping El Diablo get rid of us for good, and I just can't allow that to happen." I took a deep breath before continuing, hoping that my words were sinking in.

"I took a chance showing this to you because it is quite possible that you would go running back to the DA, protecting him because that is your job, or you can stand with us, because that is the right thing to do. Chalupa is innocent, and he always has been. I'm just hoping that you're going to do the right thing, for all of us, and for me."

She looked like she wanted to cry, like everything she'd been working so hard to achieve had just been snatched right out of her arms, and I knew exactly how that felt. We both stood there in silence for a few moments while she rewatched the video a few more times, realizing that it was authentic footage of the exchange, and she looked up at me, staring deep into my eyes to tell me how she truly felt.

"I'm so sorry, Moves," she said, and at that moment I thought that she was going to take off, that I'd made a huge mistake by trusting her with that footage, but she inched closer to me, caressing my cheek and pressing her lips up against mine.

"I'm sorry that I was so quick to judge, that you all had been dealing with this and I had no idea. I had an inkling that the man arrested had been a part of the Outlaw Souls, and that he was innocent, but I had to be sure before I could move on it. I have and always will stand for justice, and right now, we're going to have to find out a way to crack down on the DA himself," she said, and I couldn't help but let myself smile.

"You're going to help us?"

She nodded. "I'm going to do it to keep an innocent man out of prison, as well as let you know that I've forgiven you. You better find a damn good way to make it up to me for leaving me half naked on the beach for some lifeguard to find me," she added teasingly, and I pulled her into my arms, kissing her passionately so I could let her know that I was going to do just that.

"Will you come back with me to Hawk's? We need to discuss this before we tell the rest of the Outlaw Souls what's been going on. We need to be smart about this, because I'm afraid that once everyone else learns about this..."

"They're going to want to get revenge immediately, causing more problems in the process," she finished for me, taking the words right out of my mouth.

"I know you can see why we have to prevent that from happening. Las Balas is bad enough on their own, and with the DA on their side, they feel like they're untouchable. This time, we're not gonna fight back with force. This time we're gonna let the system run its course for a change, and hopefully keep Chalupa out of jail."

"I will not let your friend go to prison, Moves, I can promise you that. Let's head back to Hawk's place and we can talk about this further," she said, and I smiled, leading her back to my motorcycle. She got on behind me, wrapped her arms around my torso, and we took off into the cool, dark night.

We arrived at Hawk's place when it was nearing four o'clock in the morning, and we both knew that he would be fast asleep, but this was something that couldn't wait. I was hoping to get Lacey on our side, and now that she was going to do everything in her power to bring the truth to light, Hawk and I had to figure out how we were going to tell the rest of the Outlaw Souls, and what we were going to do to take down the DA and Las Balas at the same time.

They had absolutely no idea what was coming for them, and they truly believed that they were going to get away with wiping us out, becoming the only biker gang to reign over La Playa. But I certainly wasn't going to allow that to happen. We'd done everything we could to make a name for ourselves, to become a family, and to live peaceful lives without the worry that someone was going to try to rip us apart for their own personal gain.

I rang the doorbell a few times until a groggy, sleepy Hawk opened up, shocked to see us both standing there. After a second, though, he nodded, already knowing what was about to go down. We didn't have much time to devise a real plan, but it was certainly a start, because the only way we were going to get close enough to the DA would be with Lacey's help. Hawk went to grab us all beers while Lacey and I settled ourselves on the couch.

"Thanks, man. After the night we've had, we certainly need one," I said, handing one over to Lacey, who also thanked Hawk.

"I see you two have worked things out, and I'm glad because I got a very angry call from Mona today telling me that I needed to straighten you out for hurting her friend," Hawk joked, and we both chuckled.

"I'm sure I still deserve that, but I've promised to make it up to Lacey when this is all finally over," I said. I turned to her and leaned in to plant a soft kiss on her forehead.

I knew it was strange for Hawk to see me be so affectionate, but I could tell that there was a part of him that was pleased I had finally found love. He and I had always bickered about the fact that I was too hard, that I never knew how to treat women right, and I had blamed it for the most part on my upbringing.

I was too afraid to let anyone in because I didn't know how to deal with the hate that could potentially ensue. With Lacey it was different. I let myself feel everything with her, not allowing myself to worry about what might happen in the future, because I'd fallen for her that much. It was evident that there was still so much that we needed to talk about, but I knew that would all happen in due time, because right now we had to make sure that the people responsible for framing Chalupa were brought to justice.

I had absolutely no idea how we were going to go about bringing down the DA, but I was fervently hoping that Lacey would have some choice ideas, otherwise we were going to be stuck, and probably right back at square one. We didn't have much time to get this done, and the longer we waited, the more of a chance Las Balas had to strike, with the DA proudly on their side.

If any of the public were to ever find out how dirty the DA really was, I was sure that he would lose his job in an instant, but I didn't even know how we were going to be able to pull something like that off. It was hard enough trying to persuade Lacey that this was really happening, but there had to be people out there that would do anything to protect the DA.

I wondered if it was possible to simply go over his head entirely with this, because even though he was the DA, there were still people that he needed to answer to. I left the ball in Lacey's court, because she was going to be our best bet at getting out of this mess before anyone else from the Outlaw Souls got hurt. If anyone knew how to work the system, it would be her.

"How are we going to do this?" I asked, knowing that there were quite a few possibilities, but I wasn't sure which of them were actually going to work.

"Lacey?" Hawk asked, and we both turned to stare at her, hoping she was going to have a few answers.

"I have no idea, but if working for him has taught me anything, he's going to be really good at covering his tracks," she began, and my heart sank. This certainly didn't sound promising. "While this video is a good start, we're going to need much more than that to take him down, but I'm sitting here trying to figure out how we're going to get it. I'm still trying to wrap my head around the fact that he's been dirty this whole time."

I knew that finding that out had probably hurt her. She had worked alongside him long enough for them to form a strong professional bond, to appreciate each other's work ethic, but now the stakes were entirely different.

"I suppose we're going to have to find a way to trap him again, because we're going to need a solid confession or proof before anyone is going to see the inside of a courtroom," Lacey said, and I realized that we were all equally on edge, especially because we didn't know how much time we had, or what Las Balas was planning.

"I'm just worried that this has been in the works longer than any of us realized. They probably have a plan to take us all down, and we're going to have to figure out how to hit them back ten times harder," Hawk chipped in.

We sat there in silence for a few minutes before Lacey announced that she had an idea. "With every transaction in the city, there's a paper trail. I know the DA probably covered his tracks, but there is always a loose end lying around. What if there is some incriminating evidence somewhere in his office?"

I had no idea how we were going to find out, but this was

a challenge that only Lacey could handle. She was the only one that had any opportunity to get into the DA's office without anyone being suspicious, and that's something that we just had to count on.

"Do you think that you can really pull that off? The last thing I want is for people to start getting suspicious of you," I said to her, and she nodded.

"We're going to need more evidence, and judging from the way that man handles business, there has to be something lying around somewhere in that mess of an office of his. Once the sun comes up, you're going to take me back to work a bit early, and I'm going to convince his assistant that I need to drop something off in his office. It's a long shot, but it's all we have right now. We need to figure out how involved he is before we try trapping him. I have a feeling he's already thought through all of the major possibilities, so now we're just going to have to hit him where it hurts," she said.

I couldn't have been prouder of her, or more grateful that she was sticking out her neck for us. I hated that I had to put her in harm's way because I couldn't imagine what the DA would do to her if he ever found out that she was working with us, that she was trying to unravel the plans he made with El Diablo.

"Come on, Lacey. Let me take you home, and we can meet up in the morning when we're getting ready to take you to work so we can hopefully get one step closer to finishing this once and for all," I said, stretching out my hand, and I felt her fingers entangle with mine while we bid Hawk goodbye.

I drove her home, trying to get her there before the sun came up. We were both exhausted, but I walked her up to the door, ready to kiss her goodbye until we were able to meet again, but she unlocked the door, checking inside to make sure the coast was clear before she dragged me into her bedroom with her.

"You're not heading back out there looking that exhausted. Come on, we can sleep it off and get down to business as soon as it's time," she said, and I smiled.

It felt so nice to curl up next to her, to get some uninterrupted sleep, even though it wasn't going to be much. I was finally able to push aside my worried that something was going to happen that we wouldn't be able to control. Having her there made everything better.

She rested her head on my chest, drifting off to sleep just as the sun began to stream in through her bedroom window.

We woke up feeling even more tired than before we'd gone to sleep, but we both knew we needed the rest because we had absolutely no idea how the rest of the day was going to go. Lacey got up and headed straight for the shower, realizing that Mona was still fast asleep.

I knew that she still had yet to tell her about everything that was going on, but I was just glad that we were finally starting to move in the right direction, that we had mended our nearly broken bridge, and we were one step closer to having a future together. I could only hope that we would be able to finish this once and for all very soon, because Lacey and I had a lot of lost time to make up for.

LACEY

I got out of the shower to see a comfortably sleeping Moves curled up in my bed, and I knew that today was going to be difficult for us both. I was still trying to process the fact that the man who'd given me my job, who'd taken a chance on me and seemed to trust and respect me, was involved in such disgusting behavior.

I wondered for a moment if that was why he had put me on the case in the first place. He probably wanted to keep me distracted so that I wouldn't actually find out the real truth about what he'd been up to because he'd know that I would never be able to let it go. The DA knew me well enough to know that I was always going to stand for the innocent, that I was going to protect those that did not deserve to be put behind bars, and he'd used that against me.

It made me angry thinking that I had felt like a failure for not finding the evidence he'd asked me to seek out, and now I knew that it had probably never even existed to begin with. He had sent me on a wild goose chase, knowing good and well that I wasn't going to find anything substantial. The whole time he had just wanted to keep me distracted enough until he could snatch the case out from under me.

I knew him well enough to know that despite his dirty cop behavior, he was going to have to keep a record of his movements somewhere or somehow. There had to be evidence in that office that would help incriminate him, and even if it wouldn't be admissible in court for me sneaking into his office to find it, I knew there had to be a way to get it in front of the right set of eyes.

He'd played me for much too long, and I wondered how many of the cops in the Department were involved in this. I knew that once we had the evidence we needed, we could start devising a plan of attack, because someone was going to have to bring him down, and I wanted that someone to be me. It hurt my heart to know that I had spent so much of my time trying to help convict an innocent man, when the DA himself knew that he hadn't had anything to do with stealing that vehicle.

I could feel the blood boil beneath my skin, but I could only imagine how Moves felt through all of this. He'd been trying to protect his own from the very beginning, and I was starting to understand why he had been so apprehensive about me when I had told him I was a lawyer. He didn't know where my loyalties were, and all he was trying to do was keep his friend out of prison, especially since Chalupa hadn't done anything to deserve what happened to him.

I promised myself that I was going to help them all, that we were going to find a way to get to the bottom of this before the DA had a chance to cover his tracks. He was a smart man, but he had absolutely no idea that I had caught on to what he was doing, and that gave me the advantage I needed to get what I could and get out before anyone could suspect a thing.

Moves drove me down to the office where I got off his

bike and walked the rest of the way so no one would catch me with him. I didn't know how many eyes were on me, or how many of the people I'd seen on an everyday basis were just out doing the DA's dirty work. It made me so angry that a man who was supposed to be protecting the people of La Playa was making deals with the worst kind of people out there.

Moves had told me everything I needed to know about what kind of people Las Balas truly was, and how they would stop at nothing to get what they wanted, even if that meant sacrificing one of their own. The thought of the DA so much as having a conversation with a man like El Diablo made my stomach turn, but it ignited something inside of me that I hadn't felt for a very long time, and that was determination. I was finally back on track, and my life felt like it had purpose again. That was all I could've ever asked for, because there was a moment where I had been starting to let myself slip, where everything I'd come to know had been proved to be a lie, and I had to figure out how to bring the truth to the surface.

I was greeted by the receptionist the minute I swiped my keycard and got inside the main offices. I noticed that the DA's assistant was roaming around, but she seemed pretty distracted, and I knew that there was the possibility I could sneak past her with the ruse that I was dropping something off for the DA that no one was allowed to touch.

I ventured off into my office, making sure to stay out of sight of Richard as well, because I didn't have time for a friendly conversation. I wasn't even sure if he had been in on this too, and that would truly hurt my heart to find out, but he didn't seem like the type. Richard had been the kind of man that had always fought for what was right, and I didn't think that he would be able to stand for such malicious behavior.

I reached into my bag, pulling out a file with the word 'confidential' stamped on the front, trying to make it look like it wasn't the file that the DA had given to me at the very start of the case, and that it was something new that only he could have a look at.

I took a deep breath, moving toward the DA's office, until his assistant tapped me on the shoulder.

"Hello, Lacey. I can take that from you," she said, reaching for the file in my hand, but I snatched it away.

"I was told that I had to place this on the DA's desk, and it can't leave my hands until then. Give me a minute?" I asked.

She gave me a hard look for a few seconds, but just when I thought my heart might burst from the suspense, she finally nodded and turned away.

I made my way over to his office, opening up the door and setting the file down on his desk. Then I waited for a minute, making sure that the coast was clear before I began to search through his things. I ran through his computer files to find that his accounts were still open, and I noticed that there was quite a substantial amount of money that had been deposited within the last few days.

I snapped a few photos with my phone, knowing that this was the kind of thing I could certainly get fired for, but I didn't care. I'd promised Moves and Hawk that I would do whatever I could to bring the real criminals to justice, and to fight for the freedom of their dear friend who'd gotten caught up in the middle of all of this.

I ran through his drawers as quickly as I could, noticing that there wasn't anything else apart from the bank statements that could indicate that he was getting an obscene amount of money from Las Balas. I'd never pegged him as the type of man who would get involved with something like that, because he'd always prided himself on the fact that he always put the law before anyone or anything else. I supposed his priorities had changed over the years, or it was quite possible that I never truly knew who he really was, and this was the kind of man he had been all along.

I was blinded by it all, just trying to do my job, allowing it to consume me, and it wasn't until he'd assigned me this case that I began to realize how dirty the people in this very office could be. It made me sick to think that the DA would ever allow himself to be bought like that.

It was more money than I'd ever seen in my entire life, and I wondered what the Las Balas did to get that kind of cash and have it in a bank account, ready for a transfer. From what Moves had told me, I always assumed that they were the kind of people that didn't want a paper trail following them around, but I supposed I had a lot to learn about how powerful these biker gangs could really be if they got in touch with the right people. That thought alone scared me, because I wondered what they would do to me if they ever found out that I was slowly trying to unravel their operations alongside the Outlaw Souls.

Moves had told me a variety of terrible stories of the nasty things they'd done to get what they wanted. He explained the differences between biker gangs to me, and while the Outlaw Souls had no doubt done some questionable things in the past, they had only been trying to protect themselves. They didn't engage in the kind of criminal activity that Las Balas prided themselves on, and that was one of the only reasons I could allow myself to get as close as I did.

I believed in Moves, and I believed in the connection between us, as it told me that he was always going to be there to protect me. It made me feel safe to know that he was right outside, that he was going to wait long enough out there to make sure that I came out okay, and that nothing happened to me. I sent him a message letting him know that I'd found something, telling him that I was going to come out in a minute.

There were a lot of people in the office that still had absolutely no idea that I was even involved in this case, and that was the beauty of undercover work. I managed to fly under the radar when I needed to, and I could only hope that we managed to plan the perfect attack to take down the DA and Las Balas once and for all.

I wanted nothing more than to see them all behind bars, wishing they'd made better choices in life, and it was in that moment that I realized I did have a purpose. For such a long time I'd been working, and secretly hating my job, but now I was able to see that it would have been worth it all along if it meant that I got to save an innocent man's life.

You're not going to get away with this, and it's only a matter of time before the world knows what you really do when you're not in the office.

Staring down at the evidence on my phone, I was trying to figure out how Las Balas could come up with such an incredible amount of money. The only things I could think of were the kind of crimes that no one liked to talk about. I knew I had to talk to Moves, because he would be the only one that could shine a light on this situation as we fought to get the rest of the truth.

Right now, we just need to focus on getting more evidence. When we have enough, we can finally make the real criminals pay.

Heading back out of the office, I made my way to where Moves had been waiting for me the entire time. He meant what he said about protecting me at all costs, and I was truly grateful to him for that.

"Got what you needed?" he asked.

"I believe I have. Now let's find a way to finish this once and for all," I said, and he pulled me in close, kissing me hard, telling me that this would never have been able to happen without me, and I couldn't have been happier or more determined than I was right then.

I wrapped my arms around Moves' torso again while he drove us back to Hawk's place, and when the door finally swung open, I stared back at a face I certainly didn't expect to see.

"Mona? What are you doing here?" I asked. She opened up the door to let us in, and I saw Hawk sitting down on his couch patiently waiting for us to get back.

"I'm here because Hawk filled me in on what's going on. I'm so sorry, Lacey, I know you've been working alongside the DA for so long now. I can't imagine what it must be like to find out that he's done something like this," she said, embracing me, and as much as I wanted to dwell on the fact that the DA had played me for a fool for a very long time, I knew I had much more important things to focus on, like how we were going to expose him for his terribly disgusting ways.

"It's okay, Mona. I've learned a lot in the past twenty-four hours, and I realized that I needed to start putting my trust elsewhere. It's time that we crack down on the DA and Las Balas, I just haven't figured out how we're going to do it. I went to his office today, and I found that his bank account was still there on his computer. One look at it told me that he'd been getting an obscene amount of money in from somewhere, and I could only imagine that El Diablo paid him off," I said, addressing them all, and they nodded.

Mona turned to me, and I couldn't quite read the expression on her face, but something told me that she was already devising a plan of her very own.

"What's that look?" I asked her.

"I want to help you all out. Lacey, you're far too close to this to be the one scoping them out, and El Diablo knows that the two of you are part of the Outlaw Souls. That only leaves one person, me," she said, and I shook my head.

"There is no way in hell that I'm going to allow you to do that. Do you have any idea how dangerous that would be for you, Mona? I can't let you walk into something you're not sure you're going to be able to get out of," I explained, but she wasn't having any of it. She'd already made up her mind that this was what she wanted to do, and I knew that if I didn't give in, she was going to try to figure it out on her own.

"It's much too dangerous, Mona," said Hawk.

"All I need to do is to go to the DA and get him to show me the evidence," she said, but she didn't even know half of it.

"All we have is that little blurry video of the exchange, but it could be played off in any way, especially if the DA gets his hands on it. He's not going to show anything to anyone, but you might be able to get a confession out of him or El Diablo," I said, warming up to the idea, even though I knew that it was going to be incredibly dangerous for her to walk into the middle of something like that.

"I have all of you backing me up," Mona said. "I know that I'm going to get through this, and I have to do what I can to help. I'm sure you guys don't have much time to see this through, and if you have any better ideas, I'm all ears."

We all looked at each other, realizing that we really didn't have many other options.

"Moves, can you show Mona the video? She needs to get a good look at the two people she's going to try to get in the middle of," I said, and he pulled out his cell phone, scrolling through to find the video before placing it safely between her fingers. She watched it a few times, and I could see the expression on her face change completely. I couldn't quite figure out why that was, and when she turned to me, I realized that I had hit a nerve with her.

"What is it, Mona?"

"Is that El Diablo?" she asked, and I nodded.

"That's the same guy who was seen around my neighborhood several years ago," she said as the blood drained out of her face. "There were rumors that he was trying to sex traffic a few of my neighbors, but there was no evidence that ever came out about that. Oh my God, is this the guy I'm going to try to get a confession out of?"

I could see the fear in her eyes. She was so afraid that something bad was going to happen to her, but I rested my hand on her shoulder, letting her know that she didn't have to get in the middle of all of this if she didn't want to. I knew that Hawk wanted nothing more than to keep her safe.

"Mona, you don't have to do this. No one is asking you to do this," said Hawk, but she shook her head, snapping out of her fear.

"It's the only chance that you guys have to get this done, and I'm going to do everything in my power to help because I can't bear to see anybody go to jail for this. If the DA is involved, it's only a matter of time before they take all of you down, and you too, Lacey, when they find out that you've been involved this entire time. I'm not letting that happen, and I need one of you to show me how to best approach this situation, and how to protect myself if I need to," she said. She'd obviously decided that this was the course of action she needed to take, and I wished I could've stopped her, but she'd made up her mind.

"All right, but we're going to play this extremely safe," I said. "We're not letting you go in there without eyes on you at all times, okay? We're going to teach you everything you need to know, and as soon as you get the information you need, you're going to get out immediately. I don't want you lingering around someone like him, especially if he's truly involved in sex trafficking." I glanced at both Hawk and

Moves, who knew quite well that El Diablo was the kind of man to be involved in something like that.

"That's the kind of people Las Balas members are," Hawk said. "They don't care about who they hurt, or who they have to step on to get their way. They have built their entire gang on sex trafficking and drugs. It's time that someone did something about it. I just wish that it didn't have to be you, Mona. I don't want you walking into the lion's den without any protection." Hawk took Mona into his arms and kissed the top of her head protectively.

"You all will follow behind me, keeping an eye on me just like Lacey said," Mona assured him. "I'm going to be just fine, and I'm going to get what you all need to finally put the criminals behind bars so we can move on. Isn't that what you want, Hawk? A chance at real happiness and freedom when your friends aren't struggling to stay away from the police? If we help them now, they're not going to try to hunt you all down anymore, and that's going to be the best change the Outlaw Souls could ever see." Even though there was no guarantee of that, it was certainly a start.

I knew that she was just trying to do the right thing, but I didn't know how to process my best friend going to entice the very man who had tried to sex traffic her neighbors. It was quite possible that El Diablo knew who she was or that he'd been scoping her out for the very same thing, but we were banking on the fact that he had no idea who she was involved with.

I could see the determination on Mona's face, the same that I had felt when Moves finally told me the truth and I had made the decision to do everything in my power to help bring the criminals to justice. I needed to see them behind bars; I needed them to pay for all the torment and trouble they'd caused to people who absolutely did not deserve it.

It was only a matter of time before my best friend was

going to have to do a little undercover work of her own, and I was just hoping that no harm came to her in the process. I wouldn't have been able to live with myself if something bad happened to her, and I knew that Hawk felt the same.

"All right, how exactly are we going to do this? I'm sure you can't just waltz in there and hope that they accept you," I said, and Hawk began to explain how things worked with Las Balas.

Every story that left his lips scared Mona even more, but she had to garner as much information as possible, because it was probably the only thing that was going to keep her alive if they ever found out what her true intentions were. I looked over at Moves, who shot me a sympathetic look, like he'd felt the pain I was going through before, and I wondered how many times people he'd cared about had walked into the middle of a situation quite like this one and had never walked back out.

I hope that you're going to be okay, Mona. I don't know what I'd do if I lost you. You're the only one that's held me together this far, and I need you. I just wish there was another way, but you're right. We don't have any time left, and this may very well be our only option.

MOVES

It's nearly time for me to clue the rest of the Outlaw Souls in on what's been going on. I know they're going to be angry with me for keeping secrets, for keeping them out of the loop when I was the one that promised to be honest with them, but I had to be sure of all the facts before I brought them information that didn't turn out to be true. Now, I know who's behind this, and I know why Chalupa was arrested under false pretenses. It's time that justice is served and Las Balas, along with the DA, can finally pay for their involvement in all of this. I know the public isn't going to take too kindly to this when word gets out, but right now we just need to get that confession.

I knew that Hawk was still on the fence about letting his girl get anywhere near El Diablo, especially because he knew just how dangerous he could really be. I stayed with him for the rest of the afternoon, while he helped get Mona ready for what she was about to experience, but he made sure to let her know that she wasn't to go off on her own until we gave her the green light.

The last thing we needed was for her to get wrapped up in something she couldn't handle, and Lacey was still trying to convince herself that she could let Mona go through with this. She was also still trying to figure out how she was going to head back to the office knowing that she would have to look the DA straight in the face and not let him catch onto the fact that she knew exactly how he went about his days when he wasn't pretending to protect the city of La Playa.

I could only imagine that she was dealing with a lot, and I promised to check in on her right after I called the meeting at the Blue Dog so I could let everyone know what had been going on.

Hawk and I went down there together to find everyone gathered around with drinks in their hand, waiting for the news, and at the forefront of the crowd was Chalupa, who wanted to know more than anyone who was the person behind him getting arrested for a crime he didn't commit. I was nervous to tell them all that we learned, to let them all know that this was far from over, but I was comforted by the fact that we had a plan.

"You two have been really secretive as of late, and I've been telling everyone that it's been for good reason, but you calling us all here makes me think that you finally found some answers," Ryder said, and I nodded my head at him.

Every ear in the room perked up at the prospect of us finally being able to end this, and I stood up in front of everyone to fill them in on everything we'd learned. The video was passed around through each and every member of the Outlaw Souls, because I was going to need all of their support, especially if things got ugly.

"You've known all this time and you didn't say anything?" asked Chalupa, and I knew he had every right to be upset, but I had to make him understand that it had really been for the best.

"We couldn't come outright and tell you until we were sure ourselves, but yes, the DA is working with El Diablo. We have a plan in place to bring them both down, but it's quite possible that things are going to get ugly in the process. In the event that happens, I need to know that I have the support and cooperation of each and every one of you," I said, and they all nodded.

"We promised that we were going to get you out of this mess, Chalupa, and we plan to do exactly that," Hawk said. "You're not going to have to live another day worrying that you're going to be spending the rest of your life behind bars because we're working on getting enough evidence to prove that not only did you not have a thing to do with that stolen car, but that the DA and El Diablo were the ones that set this all up from the very beginning." I appreciated him stepping up to the plate and taking some of the heat and pressure off of me. I knew that there were the select few that were still upset that I had withheld this information from them, but they were soon going to see that there had been a good reason.

I glanced around the room at every pair of watchful eyes while they all came to terms with the fact we were one step closer to our freedom. We almost had everything we needed to make sure that the LPPD was never going to touch any member of the Outlaw Souls again, and that's all I ever wanted. I'd been enforcing the rules for a very long time, giving everyone everything they could possibly need to protect themselves, but this was exactly the kind of leadership I'd always wanted to show them all that I was capable of. I wanted them to know that they could trust me, that we were truly all in this together, and I knew it was only going to be a matter of time before this all went down.

LACEY

I hate that I have to return to the office today and pretend that everything's fine when it certainly isn't. How am I supposed to look that man in the eyes without letting him know that I've come to despise his very existence?

I was so worried that I was going to blow this for myself before I even had the chance of bringing the truth to the surface. I didn't know how to focus on anything else, and I knew the moment I sat at my desk, I was just going to spend the rest of the day plotting, hoping that Mona heeded our warnings about not doing anything without our go-ahead.

It was bad enough that she was even involved, but I was so worried that she was going to end up getting hurt or worse because of all of this. She had no idea what El Diablo could do if she said the wrong thing, or if he found out that she had been involved with the Outlaw Souls. The way that Hawk and Moves spoke of him it was quite clear that he would probably kill her on the spot from the moment he found out the truth.

I had to make sure that didn't happen, that we gave her everything she needed to protect herself until we could get the truth out of one of them.

I bid her goodbye that morning, warning her yet again about what she could be getting herself into, but she brushed it off saying that she wasn't going to try anything stupid without telling one of us first. I left the house feeling like something bad was about to happen, but I brushed it off because I knew that I had every right to feel the uneasiness in my stomach.

I had to head back to the office and pretend that everything was fine when I knew the truth. The DA was the kind of man that could be bribed, bought off by people who spent their days engaging in some of the most vile criminal acts I'd ever heard of. The DA was supposed to be the one that brought those kinds of criminals to justice, but instead he was just helping them continue to walk the streets completely unharmed.

That thought alone made my blood boil, but I had to plaster a smile on my face from the moment I walked through the door, heading straight for my office to indulge in a little work, keeping a close eye on when the DA arrived, and what he was doing in that office of his.

I made a few extra coffee trips, passing by his office every so often to make sure that he wasn't shutting his door to take any shady phone calls or communicating with the enemy right under everyone's noses. I knew he was going to call me into his office eventually, but I didn't know how to keep myself from blurting out the fact that I knew his secret, that I knew just how dirty he really was, and how sick it made me.

I could've only imagined that he would get a few deputies on me, making sure I was down before I could share what I knew with anyone, but I had to keep a straight face. I didn't want to be the one to ruin this because we were really just so close now that blowing it all would be a complete and utter disaster.

It wasn't long before the receptionist popped her head in,

telling me that the DA would like to see me in his office, and I knew I had to think on my feet, because it was quite possible he was only calling me in there to see if I was just as clueless as I had been before.

It was like he'd been using me the whole time to get close to the Outlaw Souls, to see if they were catching on to what he was doing before he had the chance to take them down himself. I kept a straight face and swallowed the anger that was welling up inside of me, because I knew it was only a matter of time before someone did something stupid or got a little too close, and that would be all the DA needed to enact his little plan.

"Lacey, have a seat," he said, and I obeyed.

"I take it you haven't found anything else that would lead us to believe that Ortega's is being used for a chop shop, right?" he asked, watching my expression carefully to see if anything had changed.

I took a deep breath and plunged in. "I don't want to disappoint you, sir, but I haven't found anything else that could point to such a lead. Any time I get close enough to anyone in that surrounding area, all I could learn was that Ortega's was in fact clean. Though I've had a hunch for a few days now that I've been missing something, that there's more that the bikers down at the Blue Dog know, and I'm determined to find out what it is. After all, we need to bring these criminals to justice."

It was a nice speech, and he smiled back at me, obviously pleased that I wasn't on his trail, even though that's exactly where I was headed. I needed him to believe that I had no idea what his plans were or who he'd been working with so he wouldn't take it upon himself to sell me out. That was the last thing I needed, and if I planned on protecting everyone that I'd come to know and love, I was going to have to convince the DA that I was on his side no matter what. It was the only way I could keep his nose out of our business.

"I have to say, Lacey. I did expect more out of you by now, but it's probably best that you take a step back from this case. I might have to give it to someone better fit for finding out the truth," he said, and I knew that he was testing me, so I glanced down at the floor, trying to get out of my head for the time being, and let him do what he wanted, because I knew it was only a matter of time before everything came crashing down around him.

"I'm sorry to hear that, sir, but I completely understand," I said, even though I didn't quite care what he thought, because I knew that this had been his plan all along. The only thing he wanted was for me to keep everyone from the Outlaw Souls distracted, trying to see if I could stir up trouble that he could use against them for the sake of Las Balas, but that wasn't going to be the case anymore.

I headed back to my office to start categorizing the few files that were on my desk because I knew I had no reason to look at them anymore, and I was just about to call it a day when I glanced down at my cell phone.

It was a text from Mona with a photo attached saying that she was at a strip club in North La Playa, and it being so early in the afternoon still, I couldn't understand what she would be doing there until I finished reading her message which said that she had seen El Diablo head in there, and that she was going to get the evidence that we needed.

I tried calling her immediately, but her phone went directly to voicemail. I didn't even know how she would've known that El Diablo was even going to be at this location, but I knew that it was probably just beginner's luck. It was either that or she'd been playing rather close attention to how

I'd been enacting my very own investigative skills. I frantically dialed Moves, waiting anxiously while the phone rang, until it eventually connected.

"Lacey? Is everything okay?"

"No! Mona just sent me a text message, that she's at some strip club where she just spotted El Diablo. I think she's trying to get the information we need, but someone has to stop her before she gets hurt," I warned, and I could feel the gears turning in Moves' head on the other end of the line.

"I was out there looking for him, canvassing the area trying to figure out where he'd gone because he wasn't at the Las Balas shop. I'm going to get Hawk, and we'll go make sure that she's safe, okay? You hang in there," he said, and I appreciated that he was going to get her, so I told him exactly what he wanted to hear.

"Thank you, Moves. I will."

I gave him no further indication that I planned on heading down there myself, because if he knew that, he would stop off at the office to try to keep me from going. I couldn't have him waste his energy on me when Mona was about to walk into something that she had no idea how to handle.

We were supposed to have more time. This was not how this was supposed to go down. I was supposed to brief her before she got anywhere near El Diablo, and now I'm afraid that we're not going to be able to get there in time.

I was so worried that El Diablo was going to see right through her, I grabbed my things and stormed out of the office, not even caring what I was leaving behind. I couldn't have imagined what was going through Mona's head right about now, because I knew there was a part of her that believed she was doing this for the greater good, and that no real harm was going to come to her, but she couldn't have been more wrong.

El Diablo was the kind of man that would stop at nothing

to get what he wanted, and that was evident, but I just didn't want him to get the chance to hurt my best friend before we could come to her rescue. She didn't deserve to be caught in the middle of all of this, and I wanted nothing more than to save her before El Diablo used her against us. If he found out that she had any connection to the Outlaw Souls, it would be over for us before we knew it.

She wouldn't have stood a chance, and I was trying to focus on anything else other than what was about to happen. We didn't have much of a plan anymore, and we were all going to walk in there blind trying to achieve the very same thing. I had no idea how to prepare for something like this, nor did I know if I was even going to walk out alive. It was anyone's game now, and I had to stay strong, keep my head held high, and focus on getting my best friend out of harm's way.

We should've never let you get involved in the first place. Mona, please stay safe until we get there. I know you think that you can do this on your own, but you can't. Please, just hold on.

MOVES

Mona, why did you have to go and do this now? This is probably the most dangerous, stupid thing you could've possibly done, and now Hawk is worried sick about you. We better get there in time to make sure that nothing happens to you, or my friend is going to spend the rest of his days unable to get over the fact that the woman he was starting to fall for died to protect the Outlaw Souls. I know how El Diablo operates, and he's going to stop at nothing until he gets what he wants. I have to get to you in time, but I have no idea what I'm about to walk into.

I revved the engine of my bike while Hawk drove alongside me. We were running out of time, and now Hawk's girl and Lacey's best friend was in an unimaginable amount of danger.

I sped up as fast as I possibly could, pulling up in front of the strip club in North La Playa, parking alongside bikes that looked a little too familiar. I knew that they were there, that El Diablo was probably waiting on the inside, enjoying his time, but he had absolutely no idea what was about to go down.

Hawk and I walked inside, and we were immediately

surrounded by women who obviously thought we were there for a good time. We politely declined, trying to focus on finding Mona, because we couldn't even imagine the kind of trouble she'd gotten herself into. The place had been crawling with Las Balas, and we tried to keep a low profile, because the minute any of them recognized us, all hell would break loose.

"Did she tell you that she was going to do this?" I asked Hawk.

"She told me that she was going to do whatever it took to get us the answers we needed, but I never thought that would mean she'd come here, to flaunt herself at El Diablo, just so she could get a confession out of him," said Hawk. I could see the hurt in his eyes, but he knew that she just wanted to be helpful.

"We're going to find her, and we're going to make sure that El Diablo doesn't lay a finger on her," I said. "If she's here to entice him, that means that we don't have long before this truly goes down. We know how El Diablo treats the women around him, and I don't want Mona to get caught up in all of that."

I knew that this was a hard pill for him to swallow, because we were probably going to have to have Mona do the very same thing she'd set off to do on her own, but it hit us out of nowhere, that we were so scared something terrible was about to happen. There was no warning, no indication that she was going to start tracking him on her own, and if we'd even begun to doubt that she would stand down until we were ready, we would've kept a closer eye on her.

I glanced around at the strippers on stage, at those that were leading men behind curtains, presumably to give them the kind of enjoyment they were looking for. I couldn't see Mona or El Diablo anywhere, but Lacey had said that they were here, so I had no choice but to keep looking. I just wanted to get in front of El Diablo, to give him hell for everything he'd put us through and make him pay for all the terrible things he'd done to the Outlaw Souls. Everyone had been right from the very beginning, suspecting that it was the Las Balas who had been behind Chalupa's arrest. I just didn't understand how a man like El Diablo could've gotten the DA on his side. The only thing I could think of was that the payout El Diablo enticed him with had to be a considerably large sum, something that man just couldn't pass up.

I hated that Lacey had to be anywhere near him, especially seeing how dangerous he was. I was so worried that he was going to catch on to the fact that she was aware of what he'd been up to lately, and I knew she was going to have a hard time getting out of that one.

I knew that she would want nothing more than for me to find her best friend, to bring her to safety, because she didn't need to be caught in the middle of all of this. I knew that Mona was just trying to do her best, just trying to keep the people she'd come to care about out of trouble, but I didn't want her to end up as another one of El Diablo's victims.

I searched for what felt forever until I noticed that someone had opened one of the back curtains to reveal a familiar face giving a lap dance to none other than El Diablo himself. The minute that Hawk caught sight of what was going on, seeing Mona there like that, made him so angry he was about to barge in and put a stop to it himself.

"Wait, wait! If you storm in there like that, Mona isn't going to get what she needs out of El Diablo, and they're probably going to kill her before you even have the chance to save her. Give it a moment. We'll keep a close eye on her to make sure nothing happens, but if she went through all this trouble to get that confession, then we have to let her see it through. We'll stay here, watch the curtain, and make sure that El Diablo doesn't lay a hand on Mona, okay?"

I could see the pain in Hawk's eyes while he tried his best

to keep his head held high, to let the woman that he loved do this for the sake of the Outlaw Souls, for the sake of keeping the people that had become his family out of jail. Mona truly was our only hope, the only chance we had at finding a way out of this, and as much as it hurt to see him like that, he knew that I was right.

If we had stormed in there, they probably would've had their guns out before we even had the chance to reach for ours, and I certainly wasn't about to let anyone get hurt because we couldn't stay still for a few more minutes. Hawk's eyes were burning through the small slit in the curtain, watching Mona do what she needed to do, but keep a safe distance away from El Diablo's hands, because she knew the minute he touched her, it would all be downhill from there. Just as we were sure she was getting him to talk, I felt a tap on my shoulder, and when I turned around I was staring at a face I really didn't want to see in a place like this.

"Lacey?"

LACEY

Why would Mona put herself through this knowing that it was quite possible she wouldn't be able to walk away? Doesn't she know how dangerous this is? When I find her and make sure that she's all right, I'm going to kill her for trying to do this on her own.

Driving down to the strip club where I was bound to run into some very terrible people, I only hoped that Moves and Hawk got there before I did, otherwise I was probably going to be facing a lot more trouble than I realized. I pulled up outside of the strip club to see that Moves' bike was parked outside, and I took a breath of relief, because at least I knew that he was in there looking for Mona.

When I got inside, the women in the room barely batted an eyelid at me. They were probably expecting a man to stroll in there with a large wad of cash to pass around, and seeing me no doubt disappointed all of them. At least they weren't going to be a distraction while I tried to find my best friend, who was off doing the stupidest thing she could've possibly thought of, even if I did know she was just trying to help.

I had told her what the stakes were, and how dangerous it was going to be for her to get involved with this before any of us had the chance to provide the backup she was most certainly going to need. I knew that Mona had been an exotic dancer back in college before we met, but I had no idea that she was going to try to use that to get what she needed out of El Diablo. We hadn't even had the chance to discuss how we planned on getting a confession out of him, but I just didn't want my best friend to get hurt.

She was strong, and she was determined, but that didn't mean that she knew exactly what she was getting herself into. I could only imagined the kind of terribly disgusting things El Diablo has done with women just like Mona, who wanted something out of him, but my greatest fear was that he'd be able to see right through her before she had the chance to get any sort of confession out of him.

She had never gone undercover like that before, and as much as we explained to her exactly what she wasn't supposed to do, that didn't mean that she was anywhere near ready to be alone with a man like that. El Diablo was a sex trafficker, he ran drugs, and he'd built his entire empire on exploiting people. I didn't know what I would do if something bad happened before I had the chance to get Mona out of there, to remind her that she had her whole life ahead of her, and that there had to be another way to do this.

I searched for what felt like forever in the rather large strip club, the heels of my boots catching on the awful red carpet and the stage lights shining overhead in different colors, creating the kind of atmosphere I didn't want to be caught in right about now. That was because I could see that the room was full of bikers who obviously didn't belong to the Outlaw Souls, and that only told me that they had to be Las Balas. We were certainly outnumbered, and I had to find Moves and Hawk before something terrible happened to me as well.

I was scared and my heart was pounding heavily in my

chest as I walked through the strip club to the very back where I saw Moves and Hawk standing there, peering into a room, and when I joined them to see what they'd been looking at, I realized that Mona was right behind the curtains. I tapped Moves on the shoulder, and he turned around to look at me, wide-eyed like he didn't expect to see me.

"Lacey? What are you doing here? I thought I told you to stay away," he said, and I shook my head.

"I know what you told me, but this is my best friend, Moves. I have to do everything I can to protect her. Is she in there right now with El Diablo?" I asked angrily, and Moves nodded.

"She's getting him to talk," said Moves, "and I know that you think she's in immediate danger, but we're keeping an eye on her to make sure that El Diablo doesn't touch her. She went through all this trouble to get a confession out of him, so if we stand in her way now, and storm in there to save her, it would all be for nothing."

"You can't just stand there and expect me to wait here while my best friend is shaking her ass for a man that is that dangerous. I don't care what the stakes are, Moves, I won't be able to live with myself if something bad happens to her, and I know that you wouldn't be able to either," I said.

He nodded. "Come here, Lacey. I need you to listen to this," Moves said, and I inched closer to him, peering into the curtain, hearing Mona getting El Diablo to finally spill what he'd been up to. It seemed that I had misjudged her, and that she was much better at this undercover work than I expected. He seemed to be quite taken with her, quite enticed by her appearance and the way she moved her body, but I could tell that Hawk had a considerably more difficult time paying attention to it all. I knew that it hurt him to see her like that, but Moves was right: the only reason she was doing this was to get that confession and protect the Outlaw Souls from crumbling to the ground.

It dawned on me that we wouldn't have anything to use as solid proof that El Diablo had been in contact with the DA, much less making deals with him unless Mona could get this confession out of him, and it surely was our last chance before everything came crashing down around us.

The Outlaw Souls were hanging on by a thread, because the minute El Diablo gave the order, I knew that the LPPD was going to start rounding up every biker that wasn't from Las Balas, and there was no way I'd be able to get all of them out from behind bars. I gulped, trying to pay attentionto what was going on in that room with my best friend, but I couldn't help but be distracted by just how angry Hawk had been.

"I need to go in there, and I need to stop her from doing this now. Please, Moves. If this doesn't go well, I can't imagine the trauma that Mona is going to have to live through after it is all said and done." Hawk pleaded with Moves, who tried to get him to understand that we were going to keep a close eye on her.

"Hawk, I understand how you feel. If it were Lacey in there now I would be storming through there ready to beat El Diablo to the ground, but he's so close to so many of his minions right now we don't stand a chance unless we manage to get him in a much more secluded spot," said Moves, and I agreed. One glance around the club told me everything I needed to know about how much danger we were in, and I was already shaking in my boots at the possibility that none of us would be making it out of here.

"Guys, I think we have a problem," I chimed in, glancing back behind the curtain to see that Mona and El Diablo were nowhere to be found.

"We need to find her. You see! This is why we should've

stormed in there a long time ago," Hawk said, brushing the curtain aside as the three of us rushed to the back where El Diablo had been sitting on the velvet tufted couch, enjoying the show.

There were drugs everywhere, and the place smelled like sweat and cheap cologne. The back area of the strip club was much bigger than I thought it would be, and that told me there were probably a lot of terrible things that were happening here that we weren't even aware of.

My heart was beating so loudly in my chest, because I had been so sure that we were keeping a close eye on Mona, that she had been right there, and nothing bad was going to happen to her, but now they were both gone. I could only hope that El Diablo didn't leave the building with her, because there would be a very slim chance we'd be able to find her after that.

I watched the boys run down the hall searching for her, busting into rooms where there were women having sex with their clients, even though that was technically not allowed. I supposed they bent the rules for some of their best clients around here, and I didn't want the same thing to happen to Mona.

I'd heard horror stories from her in the past about what she and her other friends had gone through while they were working as strippers, being coerced into doing things they much rather not do, but the men that would walk into their clubs had an incredible amount of power, making it nearly impossible for them to get out before they would start demanding more from them.

I didn't want Mona to have to relive those situations just because she wanted to get a confession out of El Diablo, because the after-effects of what that would be like for her simply wasn't worth it. I wanted nothing more than to get her to safety, and it hurt my heart that in the single moment I took my eyes off of her, El Diablo had taken her away, farther into the depths of the strip club, with a plan of his very own.

I could feel myself start to get a little lightheaded at the thought of what a majority of these women must be going through, and now that I was aware that El Diablo was heavily involved in sex trafficking, I could only imagine how many women's lives he'd stolen away from them to make a quick wad of cash. It made me sick, but I had to stay alert, because I needed to find my best friend, and I needed to make sure that we all walked out of here unscathed.

MOVES

Hawk was going to kill Lacey and me for arguing when we should've been keeping a close eye on Mona, and now she was nowhere to be found. I knew that Hawk's mind was racing with thoughts of what could possibly be happening to her, and it hurt to see him so distraught. I had promised him that no harm was going to come to Mona, that we were going to get her out before anything bad happened, but now I wasn't so sure I was going to be able to keep that promise.

We were searching for clues, trying to get into doors that were locked and resisting the temptation to bust out our handguns because the minute we opened fire in a place like this, they would have us surrounded.

We managed to fly under the radar for the most part, staying out of everyone's hair, and none of the other Las Balas members seemed to catch on to what we were doing. I couldn't understand how El Diablo had managed to get Mona out of the main area so quickly, leaving the evidence of drugs and alcohol behind, but no sign of where they could've gone.

As we traveled deeper into the back of the strip club, we happened upon a lot of rooms that had signs telling us not to disturb the activities that were going on inside, and we knew that it was just a way for some of the girls to earn a bit of extra cash.

I had a feeling that El Diablo was trying to use that to his advantage. Mona would never take it as far enough to sleep with him to get the confession, but I worried that we were not going to be able to reach her in time to keep him from forcing her.

Hawk was frantically searching through the few open rooms, glancing around at the traces of alcohol, drugs, and lingerie that littered every corner of the hallway, and I could tell that he was starting to feel sick to his stomach.

"Where the hell could they be?" Hawk asked, and I watched as Lacey ran to him, placing both of her hands on his shoulders, trying to get him to calm down.

"Listen, we're going to find them, and we're going to make sure that Mona is okay. I know that you're angry, I know that you want nothing more than to blow this place up looking for her, but we have to be smart about it. Any wrong move and El Diablo is going to have no choice but to hurt her to protect himself, and that is the last thing we want." Lacey certainly had a point.

"Okay, okay. We just need to get her back. I need to get her back," he said, and I could tell that he was starting to lose it, but I also knew that he would be able to control himself for Mona's sake. There were just a few rooms left that we hadn't searched yet, and it wouldn't be long before we had El Diablo right where we wanted him so we could get that confession and get out.

Something told me that he didn't bring his minions back here, and they were probably stationed outside for a reason, to catch any one of us strolling in asking too many questions. El Diablo had chosen the wrong venue though, because his men were far too busy enjoying the show outside to pay any sort of attention to him or protecting his little rendezvous with Mona. We just had to get to her in time, to steal her away before El Diablo really had the chance to hurt her, because we knew how terribly this could turn out.

I thought back to all the terrible rumors that had traveled amongst the Outlaw Souls, hearing the kind of things that Las Balas did without any repercussions, and it really made me sick to my stomach. To think that El Diablo believed that he had enough power to be invincible, that no one would ever be able to touch him, made me even angrier. The blood boiled beneath my skin and adrenaline coursed through me while I helped Hawk tear the back rooms of the strip club apart looking for his girl.

I knew he wanted nothing more than to hold her in his arms again, to tell her that everything was going to be okay, and she no longer had to worry, but judging from the look in his eyes, he was worried he wasn't going to be able to get that chance.

I wanted to do my part, to let him know that everything was going to be okay, but I was starting to think that El Diablo must've gotten the upper hand with this one, because it looked like he'd disappeared into thin air.

I looked at Lacey, who was so filled with determination that she couldn't let her emotions get the best of her, because I knew that she was hurting too. I would've probably acted out much worse if it had been her in there, but I was starting to think that I had made the wrong call asking us to wait, hoping that she was going to get that confession.

Now, Mona was really in danger, and there was no telling what El Diablo was going to do to her if he ever found out that she had any sort of connection to us. He was the kind of man to get rid of a threat and not have a care in the world, not even bothering to get the whole truth before he took someone out, and that's what made him so dangerous.

I didn't want Mona to have to suffer through any of that, and so we continued our search to find her.

I could've sworn I heard a noise coming from the very back of one of the rooms, the ones that were the closest to the exit, and I listened closely at the door, motioning for Hawk to join me while Lacey followed suit.

The door was locked, and it didn't seem like it was going to budge, but I listened closely to hear the conversation that was happening on the other side. It was Mona's voice, toying with El Diablo, and she was leading him right up to the point where he was about to talk.

She's going to get that confession out of him if it's the last thing she does, huh?

I moved out of the way, just as I heard Mona get what she needed, and I could've only hoped that she had some way of recording that. Hawk kicked the door down just as El Diablo began to pull at Mona's panties, trying to get her to cooperate, but we made it just in time.

"Get your hands off of her, El Diablo," Hawk yelled.

"Well, if it isn't the two of you. I thought I told my men to keep any dogs out of my club," he said, staring at us while Mona got the chance to escape from his grasp, running into Lacey's arms.

"What the hell do you think you're doing?" I asked him.

"I'm just here to have a little fun, but that tease over there hasn't been making it very easy for me. She told me she wanted to play around with a man that knew what he was doing, and then she tried to get me to stop. You two aren't going to stop me from getting to her, and I'm going to make her give me the wildest ride of my life. I just have to say the word, and every member of Las

Balas will be in here in a second to take care of you so I can continue having my nice time," he said, and the sound of his voice alone made me want to pull out my gun and shoot him.

"I don't think you're going to get that chance, El Diablo. You see, while you were caught up being enticed by our dear friend Mona over here, she managed to get a confession out of you that's going to make sure Las Balas are gone for good," I chimed in, even though I wasn't sure if she'd even gotten it recorded.

"What are you talking about?"

"You drive a hard bargain, El Diablo, but I managed to leave my voice recording running, and we finally have all we need to take you and the DA down for good," said Mona, disgusted by his behavior but enjoying putting in her two cents.

"You're going to pay for this," he said, as he was about to shout to get the rest of his men on us, but I wasn't going to allow it to happen. I reached into my pocket to pull out my knife, while Hawk kept his gun pointed at El Diablo, so he wouldn't have the chance to escape. We were alone, and far enough away from the crowd that no one would be able to hear him scream.

"Lacey, get Mona out of here. Get in your car and take her home. Don't let anyone talk to you, and don't let anyone stop you from leaving," I said, giving Lacey firm instructions so she wouldn't have to see what we were about to do. She nodded, wrapping her jacket around Mona's shoulders while she led her out, and I turned my attention back to El Diablo, who for the first time his life, knew that he wasn't going to be getting out of this one.

"I've been waiting for this moment for a very long time. Don't worry, your buddies will do just fine without you when they're all safely tucked behind bars," I said, driving the knife deep into his stomach. When he screamed, I pulled it out and stabbed him again.

He was barely hanging on to life when I stepped aside, letting Hawk fire off the final shot, making sure that he was dead before we escaped through the back door. The place had erupted into chaos while we both ran for our bikes, checking to make sure that Lacey's car was nowhere in the parking lot, and I heaved a sigh of relief when I realized they had managed to get away.

Hawk and I hopped onto our bikes, revving our engines while we drove away, just as members of Las Balas started shooting at us, but we managed to slip away before they could get on their bikes to chase us down.

I glanced over at Hawk, who grinned back at me in relief that Mona was okay, that we had managed to get to her before El Diablo had his way, and that she was going to be just fine. I knew that he was going to have quite the fight with me for how things played out, but it was truly a victory for us both, as well as the Outlaw Souls, because we now had the confession that was going to take down Las Balas along with the DA.

We had everything we needed to protect our own, to make sure that none of the Outlaw Souls were going to end up behind bars, and that was all I could've ever asked for.

I knew that they'd all been on edge for such a long time, but now we were just about to give them the good news, the news that they no longer had to fear for their lives. It was time that the Outlaw Souls got to walk free without the LPPD hounding our asses, trying to scare us into confessing to crimes we didn't commit.

There were terrible crimes that were committed, and those criminals were about to pay for their actions.

Hawk and I drove down to Lacey's house, hoping that Mona

was doing all right, but I knew that all Hawk wanted was a moment alone with her so he could tell her how sorry he was. We were all worried about her, frantically searching for her when we knew she disappeared for those few terrible moments, where El Diablo could've taken her somewhere far away from the club. It was lucky that he hadn't left the building, but I knew that Hawk would never let Mona get involved with anything like this ever again, and this time I was going to have to agree with him.

We arrived back at Lacey's house to find Mona sitting on the couch, curled up with a blanket over her shoulders, and Hawk rushed to her side. Lacey got up, leaving the two of them alone for a moment while she joined me outside. I could see the fear in her eyes start to dissipate as she realized everyone was safe again, even though there was still a bit more to be done before we could all breathe easy again.

"I'm sorry, Lacey. I know that we should've got to Mona earlier, that something terrible could've happened to her," I said, looking down at the ground, but she reached up to caress both of my cheeks, leaning in to kiss me.

"I'm just glad that we were there before she got hurt. She's going to pull through this, and even though I'm never going to let her anywhere near this kind of trouble again, she did get what we needed. All she wanted to do was help, and if we would've tried to convince her to wait, it was quite possible we were never going to get the confession," Lacey pointed out, and I agreed.

"We have it now, and that's all that matters. What are you planning on doing with it?" I asked, because we had never really discussed what would happen from here on out.

"I'm going to have to go above the DA, head straight to the mayor's office and hope that he's willing to hear me out. I don't have any reason to believe that the mayor would want to protect the DA in any way, so first thing tomorrow, we can finally put an end to all of this," she said, and I couldn't have been happier.

"Thank you, Lacey. I don't know how to show you how grateful I am that you stuck your neck out for us, that you nearly lost your job because you agreed to help."

"I would've done it regardless, because there is no way that I'm going to stand back and let an innocent man go to prison. The DA had to pay for his crimes, and now that El Diablo is out of the picture, I know Las Balas isn't going to be a problem for you anymore," she said, and I leaned in to kiss her. I felt the relief emanating from her, and I was so glad that we were nearly on the other side of this.

"I'm just glad that we got to count this as a victory, because if we were any later in finding Mona, I can't even imagine what would've happened," I said, feeling rather guilty for asking Hawk to wait, but it turned out to be for the best because if we had gone in there to rescue Mona right away, we wouldn't have had the confession, and we would probably be right back to square one.

"El Diablo deserved to die for what he's done to so many other people out there. He's the prime example of what a bad biker gang leader looks like, and while I had my doubts about the Outlaw Souls in the beginning, now all I want to do is protect you all in any way I can. I know that we've been through quite a lot together, and we haven't really had much of a chance to talk about us after everything that happened, but I need you to know how much I care about you, Moves," Lacey said.

"It's been hard for me to show my emotions, to come to terms with the fact that I'm not as broken as I always believed I was. Now, after you've come into my life, I see that I have much more to look forward to, that I didn't have to brood alone in my own darkness anymore, or try to fill the void with alcohol or meaningless relationships. You gave me something to live for, Lacey, and there are no words that can tell you how grateful I am for that, except..."

"Except what?" she asked, waiting for the three little words to leave my lips.

"I love you, Lacey," I said, and it felt so strange coming out of my mouth, but I never believed in anything more than I did that single sentence. I watched her face light up the minute she heard it, and that was all she needed to believe that we were in it for the long run.

"I love you too, Moves," she replied, and I took her into my arms, squeezing her tightly while I pressed my lips into hers, kissing her passionately to remind her that we were in this together.

I couldn't describe the feeling that had begun to well up inside me, the true pleasure that I got from hearing her tell me that she loved me, because I genuinely wanted to spend the rest of my days with her. Now, I couldn't imagine my life without her, and I was so glad that we had managed to power through the worst of this together, because it brought us closer.

We were well on our way to discovering the best parts about each other, to understand what it means to be in love. That was all I could ever ask for, and I wouldn't trade that feeling for anything in the world.

LACEY

It was the morning that we'd all been waiting for. The Outlaw Souls were all gathered at the Blue Dog, waiting to hear what the mayor had to say about the evidence against the DA, but I'd be lying if I said I wasn't nervous. There was no telling how this conversation was going to go, or if he was even going to agree to see me at all, but I had to try. After everything that Mona put herself through to get this information, it had to be brought to light, and the DA had to pay for his crimes. I couldn't wait to see the LPPD drop the charges against Chalupa, to see that he could finally return to a sense of normalcy while they start to round up the real criminals. That's all I truly needed, because that alone was going to bring me joy.

I glanced at my reflection in the mirror, while I pulled my hair back into a low bun, threw on a blazer I would normally wear to work, and looked back at the sleeping Moves on my bed, so calm and peaceful. It was the first time he wasn't tossing and turning in his sleep, and I knew he could finally rest easy knowing that this would soon be over for good.

All Moves had ever wanted was to give the Outlaw Souls

their freedom back, to show them that they could roam about without the LPPD hot on their trail because they weren't doing the kind of disgusting things that El Diablo had built his empire on.

They weren't the kind of people that would ever stand for that sort of behavior, and that was why I wanted to do more for them. In such a short amount of time, the Outlaw Souls had become family to me. They'd shown me that there was much more to life than chasing a job that I didn't even like, just so I could have something to give me a little purpose in life.

Now I knew that I could do more, that I had more power than I had ever had before, and I was going to use that to benefit the people who had done nothing but look out for me. I wanted to show them that I was grateful they came into my life when they did, because I'd truly changed because of them.

Moves had taught me to live again, he'd shown me how to let loose and be myself without the worry that I was going to get too caught up in my work to have a real, balanced personal life.

Now, he'd seen me in action, and I wondered what would happen to the DA's office once this evidence was brought to light, but I could only imagine that I wouldn't have much of a problem sticking around once he was booted out of his own office. I worried that he was going to try to enact his revenge, because I couldn't imagine that El Diablo was his only criminal contact, but I knew I was going to feel safer once he was finally behind bars.

I didn't have to worry too much or continue to watch my back because I knew that I had people looking out for me. I remembered what it was like walking into the Blue Dog for the first time and being terrified that I was about to get wrapped up in something I truly couldn't handle, but now I couldn't imagine my life without the Outlaw Souls.

I felt like I belonged with them, and before I met Moves, I'd struggled to feel like I belonged anywhere. I knew that this was going to open up a lot more doors for me, that I was going to be able to do the kind of good that I'd always wanted to do, now that I had people to fight for and protect.

I promised myself that I was going to do everything in my power to keep each and every member of the Outlaw Souls safe, because that is what they deserved. They'd been wrongfully accused one too many times, and their rivals almost got the upper hand, crumbling them for good, but we managed to take them down.

I couldn't describe the pleasure that coursed through me knowing that the real criminals were going to serve jail time for every nasty thing they'd ever done and every person they'd hurt along the way. It brought me the kind of satisfaction that made this job feel like such a blessing, because I remembered a time when all I ever did was resent it.

I gathered my things, leaning over Moves while he slept, planting a soft kiss on his lips to let him know I was heading out, and I watched his eyes flutter open so he could get a good look at me, smiling while he tried so hard to wake up.

"I didn't mean to wake you, I just couldn't leave without a kiss," I said, and he pulled me in, kissing me hard. He started to get out of bed, but I pushed him back down.

"Oh, no. I can handle this one, Moves. You and Hawk both have been going through so much trying to protect everyone around you, and you need to rest. I will be fine, and I promise that I will call you the minute this is all finally over. Please, get some rest," I begged, and he smiled, wanting nothing more than to join me, but he knew that I had a point.

"I'm going to come running the minute I get your call. I love you, Lacey," he said, and I kissed him again.

"I love you too, Moves. I will see you soon," I replied, heading toward the door and smiling to myself. I got into my car, starting up the engine while I pulled out of the driveway, making my way to the mayor's office, hoping that the receptionist wasn't going to give me too much trouble about not having an appointment, but I knew exactly what I needed to say to get my way.

My stomach was turning at the thought of how this conversation was about to go down, but I kept myself completely focused on the task at hand as I went through the metal detector and past the security guards. Soon this would be over and I could return home to Moves to tell him the good news.

"I'm from the DA's office," I told the receptionist when I arrived at the office, "and I have a matter I need to discuss with the mayor privately. It is something that I cannot discuss with you," I said, showing her my credentials. She called in to the mayor and got permission for me to enter before leading me to the double doors of his office. As she opened them for me, I could hear my own heartbeat in my ears, almost as if my heart was about to rip straight through my chest.

I had never done anything quite as nerve-wracking as this in all my years at the DA's office. I was overcome with joy and fear all at the same time, and the only thing I wanted was to show the mayor what I had in the hopes that he would believe the evidence and have the DA arrested.

"Hello. Lacey, is it? What brings you down here today?" The mayor motioned for me to sit, and I obliged, putting my briefcase down on the chair beside mine.

I took a deep breath and clenched my shaking hands together in my lap. "I don't know how else to tell you this, sir," I began, "but I was put on a case a few weeks ago by the

DA himself where he had me checking out an auto shop on the suspicions that it was chopping up cars and selling the parts illegally. A man was arrested in regard to a stolen vehicle. The DA thought he and his club were linked to the auto thefts, but it turned out that the DA was just trying to lead me on a wild goose chase. I need to show you this video and play this recording for you, because you might be aware of a motorcycle gang by the name of Las Balas? Well, the DA had quite the meeting with their leader, and this is what he had to say." I handed him my phone, letting him watch the blurry video first so he could see that something was indeed exchanged between the DA's hands and El Diablo's.

He watched it over a few times before I recounted what had happened at the strip club and played him the recording of El Diablo and Mona's conversation. When it was over, he removed his glasses, rubbing the bridge of his nose in utter frustration, trying to find the words to describe how terribly shocked and disappointed he was.

"I admire you for sticking up for the rights of the people of La Playa," he said finally, leaning back in his chair and regarding me thoughtfully. "They should not have a man like this be in charge of their safety when all he wants is a cash grab. I have to thank you for being so diligent, for fighting against the odds, and bringing the truth to light because I can only imagine that it wasn't easy getting this confession out of this El Diablo. I can assure you that the DA will be removed from his office, and we will have him arrested while we look further into this. I know it must be difficult to see a man that you once trusted get involved with something like this, but I have to say it's not my first time seeing it happen. I'm just glad that there are people out there like you who are willing to do whatever it takes to get the truth. I commend you, Lacey, and I can assure you that it will all be handed from here."

I was beaming.

"Thank you, sir. Thank you very much," I said. We shook hands and I left his office feeling like we'd just truly won. It was everything I'd wanted for such a long time, and now the people that I loved the most were all safe.

I made my way straight to the Blue Dog with the biggest smile on my face, where everyone was gathered, waiting patiently for the news. As I entered, Moves jumped to his feet, and everyone else turned to me with anxious and inquisitive expressions. I stopped and nodded my head, giving them a big smile and pumping my fist in the air.

"It's done. We did it. The DA is going down, and Las Balas won't be bothering any of you anymore," I said, and I squealed as Moves ran to me, swung me up into his arms, and spun me around, laughing in triumph.

It was the happiest we'd ever been, and we could finally rejoice as one. It was a moment that I was going to remember for the rest of my life, and Moves took me home that evening to make love to me like he never had before.

It filled me with the kind of pleasure and contentment that I had been fighting to understand the first time we'd slept together, on the beach. Now he was mine, and I was his. We had the entire world at our fingertips, and I couldn't wait to see what adventures we were going to find ourselves in next. We had everything we could ever ask for, but I knew this wouldn't be the end of trouble for us.

Moves and I had to enjoy the calm waters while we could, because I could only imagine that when one enemy gets put away, another one will eventually take their place.

That is a problem for another day, but for right now I just want to be here with Moves, enjoy this moment, and remember how long we've truly wanted this.

Epilogue: Lacey

It was like I'd finally gotten my happy ending. Everything I'd wanted from the very first time I stepped foot into the Outlaw Souls' lives was finally in my grasp. I had fallen in love with a man that had changed me, had made me a better woman, and I promised him that I would do everything in my power to make sure that everyone around us both were safe.

I had my best friend back, enjoying her time exploring her relationship with Hawk, and we all got together as often as we could to enjoy our time together now that we had no trouble or enemies to deal with. I knew that when it came to getting involved with the Outlaw Souls, that my journey would be far from over, because there was truly never going to be a dull moment again, but I was ready for whatever we had to face next.

I was sure about my capabilities now, and I knew where my priorities were, so that was why I decided to follow the dreams I'd had from the very beginning. I resigned from the DA's office after he got arrested, and since Richard had taken his place, I knew that the city of La Playa was once again in good hands. I wasn't going to be able to protect the people I loved from behind those four walls, and so I turned in my resignation and became a criminal defense attorney that worked for the Outlaw Souls.

I promised each and every member of the Outlaw Souls that I would stop at nothing to get them the justice they deserved, especially if a situation like this ever arose again. It felt good to know that the real criminals were behind bars, that the man who once had an immense amount of power was now behind bars, and that was a victory in itself.

Las Balas was under investigation by the LPPD, and we

watched in triumph as they were snatched up, one after the other, so they could serve the jail time they desperately needed to. As for their leader, he was dead, and while that was a victory for now, I could only imagine that someone was eventually going to take his place. That was how it worked in the minds of criminals, and there was always going to be someone around to threaten the people who were just trying to carry on with their lives.

At least this time, I was there to protect them all, to make sure that they had everything they needed to stand tall, to put forth a united front, and exist as one.

Just a few months ago, I never thought I would have this much happiness in my life, or this much purpose. I felt good going to work every day knowing that I was protecting the very people who had done everything in their power to keep me safe. That gave me the kind of comfort that anyone in my position would want, and I knew that the Outlaw Souls had my back.

As for Moves and I, we were finally ready to take the next step in our relationship. I brought out something in him that even I didn't realize, and it wasn't until he told me the story of his childhood that I understood why he'd been so cold and distant at one point. I knew that he must've seen quite a lot in his times with the Outlaw Souls, and he was dealing with the kind of trauma that anyone would have trouble getting past, but I was so proud of him. No matter how torn up he was, no matter how many people challenged his authority, he always made sure to stay true to who he was. I told him that there would be time to fix the relationships that had suffered because of his role in the Outlaw Souls, and it wasn't too late to find the middle ground he'd always wanted.

I sat on the back of his bike with my arms tightly wrapped around his torso remembering how I had felt the very first time he'd taken me for a ride. We were finally on our way to our own happy ending, and I watched while Moves revved his engine, driving us straight to Las Vegas. I was the one that convinced him it would be a good idea to start smoothing things over with his brother, and while he'd been a little apprehensive at first, I knew there was nothing that he wanted more in the world than to have a relationship with Keith again.

I promised that I was going to be there every step of the way and hold his hand through this tough time the same way he had for me every day for the last few months. We were growing alongside each other, and I could absolutely see myself spending the rest of my life with Moves. He'd taught me everything I needed to know about staying strong and about persevering despite how difficult things might get along the way, and I would always be grateful to him for that.

It might have been the end of one chapter, but we were just about to embark on a journey that was going to dictate the rest of our lives, and I couldn't have thought of a better way than to finally elope together. I loved Moves more than I'd ever loved anyone in my entire life, and I knew that we were going to do incredible things together.

This is just the beginning for us, Moves, and I know that no matter what life throws at us, we're always going to get through it, because we have each other's backs. You showed me that I could truly have everything I've ever wanted, and I will spend the rest of my life showing you that I will always be by your side.

You've quickly become everything I could ever ask for, and I'm never going to let go of that. I have you to thank for being the reason I followed my dreams, and I know we have a long way to go from here. I love you, Moves, and I always will.

EPILOGUE
Lacey

It was like I'd finally gotten my happy ending. Everything I'd wanted from the very first time I stepped foot into the Outlaw Souls' lives was finally in my grasp. I had fallen in love with a man that had changed me, had made me a better woman, and I promised him that I would do everything in my power to make sure that everyone around us both were safe.

I had my best friend back, enjoying her time exploring her relationship with Hawk, and we all got together as often as we could to enjoy our time together now that we had no trouble or enemies to deal with. I knew that when it came to getting involved with the Outlaw Souls, that my journey would be far from over, because there was truly never going to be a dull moment again, but I was ready for whatever we had to face next.

I was sure about my capabilities now, and I knew where my priorities were, so that was why I decided to follow the dreams I'd had from the very beginning. I resigned from the DA's office after he got arrested, and since Richard had taken his place, I knew that the city of La Playa was once again in good hands. I wasn't going to be able to protect the people I loved from behind those four walls, and so I turned in my resignation and became a criminal defense attorney that worked for the Outlaw Souls.

I promised each and every member of the Outlaw Souls that I would stop at nothing to get them the justice they deserved, especially if a situation like this ever arose again. It felt good to know that the real criminals were behind bars, that the man who once had an immense amount of power was now behind bars, and that was a victory in itself.

Las Balas was under investigation by the LPPD, and we watched in triumph as they were snatched up, one after the other, so they could serve the jail time they desperately needed to. As for their leader, he was dead, and while that was a victory for now, I could only imagine that someone was eventually going to take his place. That was how it worked in the minds of criminals, and there was always going to be someone around to threaten the people who were just trying to carry on with their lives.

At least this time, I was there to protect them all, to make sure that they had everything they needed to stand tall, to put forth a united front, and exist as one.

Just a few months ago, I never thought I would have this much happiness in my life, or this much purpose. I felt good going to work every day knowing that I was protecting the very people who had done everything in their power to keep me safe. That gave me the kind of comfort that anyone in my position would want, and I knew that the Outlaw Souls had my back.

As for Moves and I, we were finally ready to take the next step in our relationship. I brought out something in him that even I didn't realize, and it wasn't until he told me the story of his childhood that I understood why he'd been so cold and distant at one point. I knew that he must've seen quite a lot in his times with the Outlaw Souls, and he was dealing with the kind of trauma that anyone would have trouble getting past, but I was so proud of him. No matter how torn up he was, no matter how many people challenged his authority, he always made sure to stay true to who he was. I told him that there would be time to fix the relationships that had suffered because of his role in the Outlaw Souls, and it wasn't too late to find the middle ground he'd always wanted.

I sat on the back of his bike with my arms tightly wrapped around his torso remembering how I had felt the very first time he'd taken me for a ride. We were finally on our way to our own happy ending, and I watched while Moves revved his engine, driving us straight to Las Vegas. I was the one that convinced him it would be a good idea to start smoothing things over with his brother, and while he'd been a little apprehensive at first, I knew there was nothing that he wanted more in the world than to have a relationship with Keith again.

I promised that I was going to be there every step of the way and hold his hand through this tough time the same way he had for me every day for the last few months. We were growing alongside each other, and I could absolutely see myself spending the rest of my life with Moves. He'd taught me everything I needed to know about staying strong and about persevering despite how difficult things might get along the way, and I would always be grateful to him for that.

It might have been the end of one chapter, but we were just about to embark on a journey that was going to dictate the rest of our lives, and I couldn't have thought of a better way than to finally elope together. I loved Moves more than I'd ever loved anyone in my entire life, and I knew that we were going to do incredible things together.

This is just the beginning for us, Moves, and I know that no matter what life throws at us, we're always going to get through it, because we have each other's backs. You showed me that I could truly have everything I've ever wanted, and I will spend the rest of my life showing you that I will always be by your side.

You've quickly become everything I could ever ask for, and I'm never going to let go of that. I have you to thank for being the reason I followed my dreams, and I know we have a long way to go from here. I love you, Moves, and I always will.

Read on for a sneak peek of **OUTLAW SOULS BOOK 8** featuring a new Outlaw Souls member, Butch, and Sabrina, the daughter of a powerful family. She's supposed to marry the man her family picked out for her. A man she doesn't love. What was supposed to be a one night fling with Butch blossoms into something real, but she's conflicted, torn between what she really wants and her family's expectations.

Buy now!
FREE with Kindle Unlimited.

Thank you so much for reading this book. If you liked **MOVES, please leave a review for it now.**

Join My Newsletter
Click here to sign up for my newsletter for deals, sneak peeks, and more.

SNEAK PEEK! BUTCH (OUTLAW SOULS BOOK 8) CHAPTER ONE

Butch

Heads turned and gawked at me as I rode my motorcycle down the street, the loud rumble of my engine disrupting a perfect sunny day in suburban America.

Being a smart-ass, I kept a cheeky grin on my face and waved at the gawking moms and dads in their Old Navy clothes, playing in the yards with their kids. Some of them were even behind white picket fences.

My eyes took it all in from behind my sunglasses, the cookie-cutter perfection of this neighborhood where none of the houses were more than ten years old and it seemed that everyone drove an SUV or minivan. Lawns were perfectly maintained, and flower beds were free of weeds. Nothing was out of place here. Well, except for me.

In their eyes, I didn't belong here, with my leather jacket and tattoos, and that was fine with me. These people probably thought that the man I was heading to see—the one living in the two-story house nestled in the curve of the cul-de-sac—was an upstanding member of society. I was sure that he fit right in here, waving good morning to the neighbors and always separating out his recycling.

But none of that meant anything to me.

I parked my bike in the street and waited with my eyes trained on the house. John Holloway lived here, and his black SUV was parked in the driveway. I'd gone to his office first, intending to make a scene there, but I discovered that he'd gone home for lunch.

So here I was, waiting in full view of the neighbors.

When John came out of the house five minutes later in his pressed gray suit, I had dismounted my bike and was leaning against it with my arms crossed. I could have gone inside to take care of my business, but I decided to wait. I wanted to do this with an audience. This man didn't get the benefit of privacy. Not after what he'd done in one of the private rooms of the club.

John was heading straight for his car, his keys in his hand. But when he saw me, he slowed to a stop, a frown marring his features. I could see that he didn't recognize me, but that would change soon enough. Straightening, I headed his way, my boots eating up the distance between us.

"Who are you?" he asked, instinctively taking a step backward.

Anger surged as I looked into his startled face, and I gripped his lapels, shoving him back into the side of his own car.

"Please," he immediately grovelled. *Pathetic.* "Don't rob me."

I let out a humorless chuckle as his eyes darted around futilely. None of his neighbors were going to step in.

"That's not why I'm here, John," I said, whipping off my sunglasses so that he could see my face more clearly.

His brow furrowed. "How do you know my name? And what do you want? You can't do this."

He talked too much. Without warning, I reached out and slapped him with an open hand across his face. I put as much strength into the blow as I could, so that he staggered to the side.

"What the fuck, man?" he shouted, holding his hand to his face. "Did you just *slap* me?"

I could feel the eyes of the neighbors burning a hole into my back, but I didn't pay them any attention. I just kept my eyes trained on the outraged jerk in front of me.

"What's the matter? You don't like getting knocked around by someone bigger than you?"

His eyes narrowed on my face, and I finally saw recognition there. He knew exactly what I was talking about.

"You're from the strip club," he said. It wasn't a question, but I nodded.

"Yeah, asshole. I am."

John frowned, straightening, but when he tried to move away, I shoved him back into the side of his car again.

"*That's* why you're here?" he asked incredulously. "Because of Cherry?"

"Hell, yeah, it is. You slap her or any of the girls, and I slap you much harder, even if I have to come to your house the next day. Got it?"

"Come on, man." He sounded annoyed now, like I was being ridiculous. "She's just a whore."

This time it was my fist that collided with his face, and I got a deep satisfaction from the crunching sound of his nose as it broke.

"Don't ever come back to the club," I spat. I was the head of security, so I would know if he tried to show up again. "You're not welcome."

John was groaning and cursing, doubled over as he held his bleeding nose. My eyes flitted around, just to make sure that I hadn't misjudged his neighbors. I hadn't. Not a single one of them was hurrying forward to help him, and every person was watching with utter shock. Things like this didn't happen around here.

"You can't do that. I'll go to your boss," John managed to say, his voice muffled by his own hand.

I smirked. Abby would eat him alive. She owned the strip club where I worked, and she looked out for her girls. She knew that this asshole had roughed up Cherry last night in a private room, and she was pissed.

"You do that." I gave him a cold smile as I put the sunglasses back on my face. "I dare you."

The sound of a police siren cut off any reply he might have given and I stepped away from the man as the cop car came shooting down the street, nearly mowing down a kid whose dad was too distracted to pay attention. It stopped right behind my bike, blocking the driveway, and two uniformed officers stepped out.

They got here quick, but it wouldn't surprise me if they'd been called before I laid a hand on John. Just having a biker in the neighborhood was enough to make some of these people reach for the phone.

"Remember what I said," I growled at John. "This was a warning, a little payback. If you show up at the club and hurt one of the girls again, I guarantee you'll end up in the hospital."

Fear flickered across John's face, and I was satisfied that he got the message. Raising my hands into the air, I complied with the cops, allowing myself to be patted down and handcuffed without incident. I wasn't packing any heat today, knowing that this might happen. As I was put into the back of the police car, I saw John answering questions while holding a rag up to his still-bleeding nose. I hoped it hurt.

When Cherry came out of the private room last night, she'd gone straight backstage without saying anything, which was why I'd allowed the man to leave. It wasn't until one of the other girls came and got me because she was crying in the dressing room that I found out he'd gotten violent with her when she refused to have sex with him. The girls were strippers only. It was a part of the club rules. If they *wanted* to exchange sex for money, it had to happen outside. Abby covered her ass that way.

John didn't go as far as to force her, but he did push her around and slap her face. I could see the bruise on her cheekbone when we talked. Abby wanted to light his ass on fire, but I talked her into letting me take care of it.

So I had. A trip downtown to lockup was worth it.

I settled into the backseat of the cop car, trying to get as comfortable as I could with my hands cuffed behind my back. There were even more neighbors outside now, a group of lookie-loos that needed something to gossip about for the rest of the day.

They could speculate all they wanted, painting me as a bad guy that had attacked one of their upstanding citizens. I didn't care. I knew who I was and what was important to me. If I had to, I'd do it again. The man needed to be taught a lesson.

SNEAK PEEK! BUTCH (OUTLAW SOULS BOOK 8) CHAPTER TWO

Sabrina

"Where are you going?"

I stopped dead in my tracks, just a couple feet away from the front door. I'd *almost* gotten away without a lecture.

Biting back a sigh, I turned around to see my mother standing at the foot of the stairs. She scanned my outfit and makeup-free face, not bothering to hide her disapproval at my appearance. Not surprising. According to Virginia Barnett, sneakers were *only* for the gym, and I'd never even seen her in a pair of jeans.

"To the soup kitchen," I said, exasperated. It was the same place I went every Friday and Saturday afternoon. That was when they had the least volunteers, but I didn't mind spending my weekend there. I also went a couple of times during the week when they needed help.

She frowned. "You're still doing that? Why?"

"Did you need something from me?" I asked.

It was easier to get straight to the point, instead of trying once again to explain to her why I spent my time feeding people in need. If she didn't get it by now, she never would.

The strange thing was that she was the one who'd introduced me to the place, but for her, it was just a photo opportunity. Taking pictures of my whole family serving meals around Christmas time last year had painted the perfect heart-warming image. The media didn't need to know that I was the only member of my family that actually cared about helping these people. All they needed to see was a senator with his seemingly perfect family giving back to the people whose votes he needed in the election at the end of the year.

"Well, I was hoping to get some help planning the dinner party next week. This is important, you know. Some of the biggest contributors to your father's campaign will be there."

"It's just a dinner party, Mom. How much is there to really plan?"

Her eyebrows popped and she crossed her arms over her chest. *Great, I've made her mad.*

"That's quite an attitude you have there. I guess I'll just do everything myself then. Plan the menu, pick a signature cocktail, take care of décor..." She trailed off and turned away from me, as if hiding her face. "I just thought it would be nice to do it together."

And there it was. The guilt trip.

If there was one thing my parents both excelled at—other than refusing to factor my own happiness into their expectations for me—it was making me feel guilty anytime I didn't fall in line with what they wanted. The twisted part was that I knew they were doing it, but I still let myself give in to the detrimental feeling that they provoked. I knew I shouldn't let them play me like that, but they were my *parents*. I wanted to make them proud of me. The sad thing was, I wasn't sure that I ever had.

"Okay, Mom. I'm sorry. I'll help you plan the dinner party. Maybe we can go shopping for new dresses together tomorrow? But right now, I've got to go to the soup kitchen. They're expecting me."

"That's fine, I guess," she agreed, letting out a long-suffering sigh.

I felt a flicker of annoyance. I'd given in to what she wanted, and I was still the bad guy because I was going to feed the poor. It was maddening.

"I'll be home later," I said, purposely being vague. My best friend, Lacey, wanted me to come by her place when I was done in the soup kitchen. My parents didn't necessarily approve of her, she was too free-spirited for them, so I didn't mention it.

Leaving the house, I drove my Lexus across town, watching as the houses changed from the grand manors of the neighborhood where I lived with my parents to more modest homes and eventually neglected houses and empty lots. The soup kitchen was nestled in the center of the seediest part of La Playa.

The building was a former Mexican restaurant. When it had gone out of business, it had been left a total mess. It had enabled the founders of the soup kitchen to obtain the property cheaply, even though there was plenty of work to be done.

I hadn't been around in those early days—I was still a teenager then—but the place had been in operation for seven years and there were still things about the building that were reminiscent of the restaurant that had been there before. The outline of the original sign on the front of the building was still visible, despite the lettering being removed, and on the inside, the floor was covered in Mexican Talavera tile. The bar had been taken out, allowing for more seating to be installed. Now it was a large, open space that could hold around a hundred people.

A few small changes could make the place much nicer, but

that was secondary to the mission on the La Playa Soup Kitchen. Any money that was raised went toward feeding as many people as possible. The tables and chairs had been donated, so they were a mismatched hodgepodge of styles and colors, but they functional, which was all that mattered here. As long as people had a place to eat, no one cared if the chairs matched.

Parking on the side street nearby, I popped my trunk, where I'd stashed a box of non-perishable food. Most of the food for the soup kitchen's pantry came from donations, and I liked to contribute as much as possible.

Carrying the box with both hands, I made my way to the entrance. The door was pushed open just before I reached it, and I was greeted by the smiling face of Sean Haggert, the man that ran the place.

"Hey, Sabrina," he said, stepping forward to take the box from me.

Sean was an Army veteran that had fought in the Gulf War. He'd had a hard time adjusting when he'd returned from overseas, and the lack of support for PTSD had resulted in a downward spiral that had ended with him self-medicating with alcohol and losing everything. He'd lived on the streets for ten hard years and it was his own experiences that made him so good at this job. He remembered what it was like to be one of the people that we helped here.

Sean shared his story with everyone, showing that he was unashamed of the darkest time of his life. I admired his strength, turning his life around and dedicating himself to helping others.

"I was starting to get worried," Sean told me as I followed him to the kitchen. "You're never late."

"I got caught up talking to my mom. You know how she can be."

He'd met her at Christmas, at the same time he'd met me, so I didn't need to elaborate. She left an impression.

The kitchen was the most up-to-date part of the building since that was where the food was prepared. Certain standards needed to be met. There was a double oven, two deep fryers, and a steamer. Stainless steel tables provided the work surface and an industrial dishwasher stood in the corner.

Another volunteer, a woman named Annie, was already there, cutting vegetables. I didn't know her well yet, since she'd only been coming for the past two weeks, but I smiled at her warmly.

Checking the menu, I saw that we were making chicken and wild rice today. The menu changed depending on the food that had been received. I'd been surprised over the last few months to find that the food could be of very high quality, depending on who donated it. Once, a seafood restaurant had overordered and donated their excess inventory to us. We were given the ingredients to allow us to prepare lobster linguini.

As I set to work, prepping the chicken to be baked and putting the rice into the steamer, I felt myself relaxing, moving with a rhythmic ease that I possessed only in the kitchen. This wasn't exactly my dream kitchen, though. That would be in a little restaurant with me in a chef's jacket. It was what I really wanted to do with my life, but instead of going to culinary school, I'd attended the University of California and studied political science. It was what my parents expected of me.

Now I made up for it as well as I could by cooking at home, which required working around whatever diet fad my mother was trying out, and by preparing food here. I was allowed some creative freedom with the menu here, cooking whatever desserts I wanted to make with the food available. I got the chance to show off by creating unique dishes.

By the time we opened for dinner two hours later, there was already a line of people outside. I loved serving my food to people, but I hated seeing so many unfortunate souls that couldn't afford to feed themselves. The children were the worst. I could see the stark hunger on their faces, as they weren't able to hide it like the adults that clung to their dignity. The soup kitchen was open seven days a week for dinner only, so that meant that this was the only meal that most of these people got in an entire day.

And my mother asked why I came here. How could she not understand?

Annie and I served the food in a cafeteria-style setup with the pans of food being kept warm on a steam table. The line formed, with every hungry person holding their trays out to us to be filled. Meanwhile, Sean worked his way through the room, interacting with everyone in the dining area. He cleared plates and washed dishes as needed, providing a welcoming presence for our guests. We worked as a unit in the chaos as the place filled up.

When we were finally done, everyone had been served and we were down to our last pans of food. I looked around the room with a feeling of pride swelling within my chest. That was the real reason that I kept coming back here. Helping these people gave me a satisfaction that I'd never known before. I was making a difference here, helping people. Of all the galas, silent auctions, and dinner parties I had attended that were designed to raise money, I'd never felt like I was really doing anything worthwhile for a cause before I found this place.

I glanced to my right and saw Annie scanning the crowd with a crease forming between her brows as she nibbled on her bottom lip. She'd been quiet all day.

"Everything okay?" I asked, putting lids on the food to keep it from drying out under the heat lamps.

"Yeah," she said absently, not turning to look at me.

I wasn't buying that.

"You sure?" I pushed, turning to face her directly. I wasn't one to beat around the bush, and this wasn't the first time I'd noticed Annie doing this. Her focus on the people here wasn't casual. She was looking for something.

She looked at me this time, and when our eyes met, I saw sadness in the lines of her face. Annie was about ten years older than me, in her early thirties, and I knew she had a young son, but other than that, we were practically strangers. Despite this, I moved close to her and placed a hand on her forearm.

"Can I help you in some way?" I asked.

Shock radiated through me when she swallowed hard and tears filled her eyes. I glanced around and saw that no one else had come in for dinner in the time we had been talking, so I guided Annie back to the kitchen to continue the conversation in private. Once we were alone, she took a shuddering breath and blinked a few times. Once she had herself under control, Annie let out a sigh.

"I'm looking for my brother," she confessed.

I wasn't exactly surprised. It fit with her behavior and the anxiety coming off of her in waves.

"He's homeless?"

She nodded. "Lance is schizophrenic. He lived with our parents, but he hates taking his medication, and last year, he got tired of fighting with them about it. He just left."

"With nowhere to go?"

"He didn't really have anyone in his life other than us. The schizophrenia drove everyone else away."

Her voice was brittle and my heart ached for her. Of course she'd come here to look for him. If he was living on the streets of La Playa, there was a good chance he'd show up at the soup kitchen.

"You have a picture?" I asked.

Annie reached into her back pocket and pulled out a wallet-sized picture of a man closer to my age with shaggy brown hair and a nice smile. He didn't look familiar to me.

"I don't think I've seen him," I said regretfully. I started to hand the picture back to her, but she shook her head.

"Keep it, please. Just so you have something to reference if he comes in when you're here. I have about a hundred more copies, just in case."

I pocketed the picture and gave her a small, encouraging smile.

"Sean's the one you want to talk to," I told her. "He's here all the time. If Lance comes in here, he'll know it."

"Thanks, Sabrina," Annie said. "I'm sorry to get so emotional. It's just...it's hard to talk about."

"Hey, don't be sorry about that."

I was sure that I'd be pretty upset too, if I were in her situation, but I was an only child.

The kitchen door opened and Sean pushed in a cart loaded with dirty dishes. "You guys hiding in here? A family of four just came in."

"On it, boss," I said, giving him a salute before pulling Annie out of the kitchen while he chuckled.

It was business as usual as we finished up the dinner, serving the stragglers for the last fifteen minutes of our hour-long dinner service and then cleaning up. But I couldn't stop thinking about Annie's brother. The poor man might not even realize that he had a loved one looking for him if he was an unmedicated schizophrenic. I glanced over at Annie as we worked together to wipe down the tables and chairs in the dining room, and I silently promised myself that I would do anything I could to help her. Someone that loved her family so much deserved answers.

I can't wait for you to find out what happens with Butch and Sabrina...

**Purchase BUTCH (OUTLAW SOULS BOOK 8)
FREE with Kindle Unlimited.**

ALSO BY HOPE STONE

All of my books are currently available to read FREE in Kindle Unlimited. Click the series link or any of the titles to check them out!

Guardians Of Mayhem MC Series

Book 1 - Finn

Book 2 - Havoc

Book 3 - Axle

Book 4 - Rush

Book 5 - Red

Book 6 - Shadow

Book 7 - Shaggy

LEAVE A REVIEW

Like this book?
Tap here to leave a review now!

Join Hope's newsletter to stay updated with new releases, get access to exclusive bonus content and much more!

Join Hope's newsletter here.

Tap here to see all of Hope's books.

Join all the fun in Hope Stone's Readers Group on Facebook.

ABOUT THE AUTHOR

Hope Stone is an Amazon #1 bestselling author who loves writing steamy action packed, emotion-filled stories with twists and turns that keep readers guessing. Hope's books revolve around possessive alpha men who love protecting their sexy and sassy heroines.

Learn more about all my books here.

Sign up to receive my newsletter. You'll get free books (starting with my two-book MC romance starter library), exclusive bonus content and news of my releases and sales.

If you liked this book, I'd be so grateful if you took a few minutes to leave a review now! Authors (including myself) really appreciate this, and it helps draw more readers to books they might like. Thanks!

MOVES: AN MC ROMANCE
Book Seven in the Outlaw Souls MC series
By Hope Stone

© Copyright 2020 - All rights reserved.

It is not legal to reproduce, duplicate, or transmit any part of this document in either electronic means or in printed format. Recording of this publication is strictly prohibited and any storage of this document is not allowed unless with written permission from the publisher except for the use of brief quotations in a book review.

This book is a work of fiction. Any resemblance to persons, living or dead, or places, events or locations is purely coincidental.

Printed in Great Britain
by Amazon